NO SUCH
PERSON

NOVELS BY CAROLINE B. COONEY

The Lost Songs
Three Black Swans
They Never Came Back
If the Witness Lied
Diamonds in the Shadow
A Friend at Midnight
Hit the Road
Code Orange
The Girl Who Invented Romance
Family Reunion
Goddess of Yesterday
The Ransom of Mercy Carter
Tune In Anytime
Burning Up
What Child Is This?
Driver's Ed
Twenty Pageants Later
Among Friends
The Time Travelers, Volumes I and II

THE JANIE BOOKS

The Face on the Milk Carton
Whatever Happened to Janie?
The Voice on the Radio
What Janie Found
What Janie Saw (a digital original short story)
Janie Face to Face

THE TIME TRAVEL QUARTET

Both Sides of Time
Out of Time
Prisoner of Time
For All Time

NO SUCH PERSON

PERSON

CAROLINE B. COONEY

DELACORTE PRESS

Text copyright © 2015 by Caroline B. Cooney
Jacket art copyright © 2015 by Tasha Marie
Interior photographs courtesy of the author

Visit us on the Web! randomhouseteens.com

Educators and librarians, for a variety of teaching tools, visit us at RHTeachersLibrarians.com

Library of Congress Cataloging-in-Publication Data
Cooney, Caroline B.
No such person / Caroline Cooney.
pages cm
Summary: "A murder mystery in a small town raises suspicions when a member of a well-regarded family in the community is implicated"—Provided by publisher.
ISBN 978-0-385-74291-7 (trade hardcover) — ISBN 978-0-375-99084-7 (library binding) — ISBN 978-0-307-97952-0 (ebook) [1. Mystery and detective stories. 2. Murder—Fiction.] I. Title.
PZ7.C7834No 2015
[Fic]—dc23
2014025075

The text of this book is set in 13.5-point Perpetua.
Jacket design by Torborg Davern
Interior design by Heather Kelly

Printed in the United States of America
10 9 8 7 6 5 4 3 2 1
First Edition

Random House Children's Books supports the First Amendment and celebrates the right to read.

It began one summer on the river. . . .

At first the police are casual.

She too is casual. Puzzled, but not worried.

The questions become more intense.

The questions frighten her.

Where are the police going with this? They are not giving her time to think. Her tongue is dry and tastes of metal. Her hands are damp. Her breath is ragged.

They're asking her about the boat. About the ownership of the boat. About the river. About the woods.

It's difficult to swallow. Her voice rises in pitch. The police seem pleased by her fear.

They have found the gun. They are holding it in a handkerchief. The crisp white cotton hangs down and the small dark weapon is thrust into her face for identification.

They are standing too close to her, but she cannot back away. There is nowhere to go.

"Yes, but it was just target practice," she says. She looks into the woods beyond the police officers. The towering trees are thick with vines and undergrowth, noisy with the clamor of insects. The heat of the day is crushing. Does she really prance into those woods? Hold a real gun and shoot a real bullet?

She is blinded by the horror of what they are saying now.

She stares at the gun. It is small and stubby. It will have her fingerprints on it. Her palm print.

"That's impossible," she whispers.

It is not impossible that a gun could kill. It is not impossible that the police have found a body. The impossible part is that she has anything to do with it.

"Red bandanna," she explains, gulping air into her lungs. "We tied it to a tree. For target practice."

She has never touched a gun before. She is anti-gun. She believes that people who own and use guns are sick and must be controlled. She would never live in one of those states where people shoot for the fun of shooting. Only people in the army should use guns and even then, they should only be peace-keepers.

But there she was, a few hours ago: giggling, happy, flirting, going along with the idea. Using the gun herself.

They want to know more about him.

She gives them his name and is frightened by how little

else she knows. How few facts she can come up with. This is impossible. Of course she knows something about him.

They feel the same. *Of course you know.*

She shakes her head. It does something to her body. Now she's shaking all over.

They want her to come with them. She cannot seem to coordinate her feet. They pull at her to get her going. She is horrified by their hands on her. She draws her elbows in and hunches down. Her teeth are chattering.

She wants to see the dead person, but they won't let her. It's a crime scene, they explain. They imply that she has already seen it.

No! she thinks. There was no one there. It didn't happen.

The police stare at her. Their eyes glitter. She is a fawn surrounded by wolves.

She and the police walk up a path. She has not noticed the path until now. The salt marsh is on her right, the reeds taller than she is. Impenetrable. Quivery in the wind. The woods are on the left. The ground is low-lying and often flooded, so debris piles up against the tree trunks.

She can barely find a place to put her feet, never mind her thoughts.

This cannot be happening.

She is a good person. A moral person. A successful person.

Someone in the woods is dead by gunshot? They must be wrong about that.

There was nobody there, she tells herself. I didn't shoot anybody.

They have reached a road. She is surprised to find pavement so close. Coming by water, the place seemed so remote. She doesn't recognize the road, which is confusing, because she is a local. It must be someone's driveway. But she sees no house. Instead she sees a police car. Parked behind it are two more police cars.

They open the back door of the cruiser. The back is where prisoners go. They are opening that door for her. She stops walking. She tries to grip the soil with the bottoms of her sneakers.

The female officer asks what is in the pocket of her Bermuda shorts. "Is it a weapon? Anything sharp?"

It is her cell phone, of course. They do not let her pull it out. They take it.

Her hand actually aches for the weight and texture of that little rectangle. The cell phone is her best friend. It never lets her down.

Now it is evidence.

She has not agreed to this. She will be lost without her phone. She must have it back. She reaches to retrieve it, and they glare at her as if she is overstepping the bounds, to want her own cell phone in her own hand.

They tell her to get into the back of the police car.

Rarely in her life has she even been nervous. Now fear owns her, like a dog holding a duck in its teeth. She shoves at the fear, but it is a police officer she is hitting. They take her arm. Not roughly, but as if it is theirs. She tries to pull free. They're too strong.

They shout at her to calm down and behave.

No!

Nothing will make her get into that police car. This is not her life! This is not—

They grip her shoulders and elbows. They pull her arms behind her.

They are going to put handcuffs on her wrists.

She doubles over, drags them down, tries to head butt them.

They are shouting in her ear, deafening her, trying to knee her into the car.

She is screaming, kicking. She would bite them if she could.

"Stop it!" they yell at her.

She is an animal. Intelligence, knowledge and poise are gone. She who dislikes bracelets, can't stand the jangle, is irritated by how they slide up, slide down—she now has bracelets that cannot be removed.

They tell her to be good; to cooperate. Act your age, they say, as if she is having a tantrum in kindergarten.

She fights so hard it takes four of them to trap her in the backseat of the police car, and before they are done, they have also fastened her ankles together with a padded Velcro strip, like a massive Band-Aid.

They close the door.

The brutal metallic slam shuts her up. She stops

screaming. She doesn't look left or right, up or down. She freezes, hoping it will all go away, like a shadow in the night.

I won't cry, she tells herself.

But she does.

The tears stream down her face. She has no tissue. She can't even use her short sleeve because of the way her wrists are fastened.

There is so much horror in her mind that she can't arrange it; can't assess it. Pieces of nightmare fly in her face like the wings of vultures; like carrion birds eager to chew on her flesh.

Who is dead?

Why do they think I did it?

Are they right?

What if they are right?

Am I a killer?

SATURDAY MORNING

The cottage is close to the edge of the bluff. The steep river-bank is rough with stubby willows, pricker bushes and one massive oak. Long rickety stairs in need of painting lead forty feet down to a skinny dock, more of a shelf really, where their Zodiac, a rugged flat-bottomed rubber-raft-type boat from which they fish and swim, bumps gently in the wake of a passing powerboat.

There are only a dozen houses on this part of the Connecticut River. They are cut off on the south by a tidal marsh filled with islets of pine and rock, and on the north by a ravine, impassable because of a tumbling brook and a fall of glacial rocks. The Allerdon cottage is the only house at the very edge of the river. Several houses are hard by the narrow country road and a few are across the road, tucked among rocks and crags. Those houses have no river access, but wonderful views.

The big screened porch juts out from the back of the Allerdon cottage, almost hanging over the river. They often refer to the cottage as a screened porch that handily comes with a kitchen and bath.

They have been awake since the first bass boat streaked down the river for the opening of a tournament.

Miranda's father has made an enormous pot of coffee. He is on his third cup, not awake from the caffeine, but happily comatose with relief that he does not drive into the office on Saturdays.

Her mother is still sipping her first cup. She is curled on the chaise with the neighbor's dog, Barrel, who comes over every morning for his own coffee. He likes milk and extra sugar.

Miranda is doing nothing, which is what summer is for. Her only plan for the entire day is to take Barrel for a run.

The neighborhood boys will be over at some point during the morning. Henry and Hayden Warren, who are seven and six, always show up. Jack, who is twelve, will come, hoping that Miranda is baking. She might. She loves to bake. And baking is cheerful proof that she is not wasting the entire day. Geoffrey, who is her own age, will lumber noisily through the bushes. It's a neighborhood thing or maybe a boy thing: never use the driveway if you can push through the shrubbery. Geoffrey will fish off their dock or maybe play catch with Miranda's father, a mindless activity they both love. Stu, whose house is highest on the hill, and whose parents have let the trees in front grow up so high they hardly have a river view anymore, may put his kayak in from their dock. Stu is a little too old to be called a boy, but each year he attends and drops out of yet another college, which seems to keep him young. Stu has a long-term crush on Miranda's sister, Lander.

Lander of course is achieving things. Lander is twenty-two, having finished college in the same blaze of glory with which she finished high school. In a few weeks, she is going on to medical school, where she will become a surgeon. This is perfect for Lander, who has a cutting-edge personality. Miranda is seven years younger than her sister, and their lives have never really intersected.

Miranda is surprised to find herself up and around. During the summer she doesn't usually get up until lunch is in sight.

Lander, however, rarely goes to bed before one or two a.m., and is up at dawn. Her agenda is long and fierce, and Lander completes everything in a timely fashion. Right now, Lander is gazing at the screen of her laptop. Although Lander does play many games, she is probably studying. Lander has already finished one e-textbook for a course that won't begin until next month.

Henry and Hayden, still in their pajamas, gallop across other people's backyards, whoop hello and throw open the screen door. There's a door at each end of the long porch and the slap of wooden doors against wooden frames is one of Miranda's favorite summer sounds. Miranda hugs the boys. It's a lot like hugging Barrel. The dog sheds and drools; Henry and Hayden are sticky and damp, having just had cereal, spilling the milk on themselves. The boys often spend the night in the Allerdon cottage so that Miranda can babysit without going anywhere. Henry and Hayden love dragging their sleeping bags across the grass and staying out in the screened porch with Miranda. There are always big plans for learning stars and constellations, but nothing ever comes of it because they instantly fall asleep.

Lander is not a fan of grubby little boys. She retreats to the kitchen.

Out in the water, the Saturday circus is on.

There are powerboats, sailboats, Jet Skis, kayaks, canoes and one raft. The river is very wide here. A few hundred yards out, a small powerboat tows a boy learning to water-ski. Miranda picks up the binoculars. The driver of the boat and the boy on skis are shirtless and muscular. They are far and away the best scenery on the river.

The boy driving the powerboat—which is called the *Paid at Last;* it is amazing to Miranda that people would squander a wonderful boat-naming opportunity by calling it after their finances—is dark-haired, and his hair is wet, and his body gleams, perhaps with sunblock. The boy in the water is blond and has no idea what he is doing. The few times he does manage to stand on the skis, he immediately falls back in the water.

The boat driver circles, giving advice, making sure his

friend has a good grip on the tow rope, and then accelerates again, hoping for success.

To Miranda's amazement, Lander produces a plate of toaster waffles for Henry and Hayden to share. The boys are ardent with gratitude. They slosh rivers of syrup over the waffles and eat with their fingers. Lander walks over to Miranda and extends her hand for the binoculars, like a surgeon extending her palm, expecting the nurse to put the proper scalpel in the proper position.

Miranda would like to tell her sister that the way to acquire the binoculars is to ask courteously for a turn. But Lander doesn't operate like that. Every encounter with her older sister requires Miranda either to confront Lander or submit to her.

Lander hasn't been home much in four years. Once she leaves for medical school, she really won't be home much. The last thing their parents want during the final month of summer is bickering, so Miranda doesn't start anything, although there is something so satisfying about bickering. No one can ever win; it's like tossing a baseball back and forth.

Miranda hands Lander the binoculars. Lander does not say thank you, because Miranda is just a little sister, not a person.

Miranda feels the usual stab of regret that she and her sister are not friends. They aren't enemies. They just aren't close and she has never figured out how to solve this.

She goes to the other end of the porch, where the scope sits on a tripod, focused on an osprey nest across the river.

They have watched several generations of fish hawks rear their young, catch their fish, hang out on their snags and sail in the wind. But Miranda is not interested in nature, although it's nice to have around. Miranda is interested in people. Right now, she is interested in the two handsome male people on display in the water.

She refocuses the scope.

The two young men are laughing. She can't hear them over the sounds of many boat motors but she laughs with them. Miranda loves laughter. She believes that Lander doesn't laugh enough, but although it is fine for the older sister to tell the younger one how to improve, it never works when the younger sister tells the older one how to improve.

The young man driving the powerboat wears baggy shorts and no shirt. The young man water-skiing wears tight black swim trunks and a large silver-and-blue flotation device. Both have fairly long hair, the wet fair hair of the skier plastered to his skull and the dark hair of the driver blowing in the wind.

"I pick the driver," says Lander, smiling at Miranda, and Miranda melts, because attention from Lander is so infrequent. "Okay," she agrees. "I take the water skier."

"He isn't one, though," points out Henry. "He can't do anything." Henry has been water-skiing since he could stand.

There really should be a second person in the powerboat so that one person can look ahead and make sure they don't collide with a dock, another boat or a swimmer while the other person keeps track of the water skier. But safety is boring and these two do not look boring.

Downriver, the tip of an oil barge appears, coming around the bend. The Connecticut River is navigable for many miles inland, but there isn't much commercial use of the river anymore. Fear of oil spills has cut it down. It takes fifty-five truckloads of oil to equal one barge, so Miranda feels it's more efficient to use barges, but most people feel that barges are too dangerous for the river. They're winning. Miranda will be so sorry when the last tug pushes the last barge upriver from Long Island Sound.

She swings the scope toward the barge, waiting for the tug to be visible. The tugs are red and blocky and sturdy. They have girls' names, like Bridget or Mary Claire, and are mostly from Staten Island, and someday Miranda plans to go to Staten Island and see if she can get a job.

The Connecticut River is wide and shallow, full of sandbars that catch the debris from storms. The channel itself is narrow, and not in the center, but quite close to the Allerdon side. Barges usually come upriver at high tide, when water from the Atlantic Ocean rushes inland for fifty miles, and the tug won't have to fight the river.

The high red tower of the tug appears behind the barge. A barge is roughly the size of half a football field and the captain has to be up very high to see over it. Even so, he cannot see the water directly in front of the massive barge; he can only see where he is going.

Miranda likes to wave at the captains, who always toot

back, so she leaves the porch, the little boys chewing waffles and her parents silent over coffee and weekend thoughts, and runs outside on the grass.

The tug whistles. It's the *Janet Anne*.

Miranda jumps up and down like a little kid. In fact, she is little; five feet two compared to her sister's elegant, slim five feet ten.

Lander follows her outside. "He's not whistling at you," says Lander. "He's warning those water-ski guys. They're right in the channel." Handing the binoculars to Miranda, Lander races down the steep steps to their narrow dock, screaming at the guys in the water. There must be too much engine noise for them to hear her words of warning, because they just wave.

The boy driving the boat circles back. The boy in the water reaches for the towline.

The tug's whistles are longer now—shrill and disturbing. But the sounds do not disturb the water-ski pair.

Miranda's father is now standing at the edge of the bluff waving his arms, semaphore style. "You don't have time for that!" he shouts. "Pick him up! Get him in the boat! Get out of the channel!"

Forty feet below, on the dock, Lander picks up a big striped beach towel and flaps it to attract attention. "Forget the skis! Get in the boat!"

Miranda cannot believe that the two young men don't react. Perhaps the screaming tug whistle, the clanking barge and the racket of their own engine have deafened them. Or perhaps they know exactly what is happening, and are betting they can outrun the tug; that it will make a wonderful video—the great black wall of the massive barge bearing down; the water skier mastering the skill at the last possible second.

Playing chicken with an oil barge is insane.

The *Janet Anne* is no longer whistling. A terrifying Klaxon begins, which in all these years summering on the river Miranda has never heard.

The tug reverses engines. The water churns. But the barge does not slow down. There are no brakes on a barge. A barge needs two miles to stop.

Miranda's mother is holding the two little boys by their pajama tops, for fear that Henry and Hayden will dive-bomb into the river and swim out to save the water skier.

The *Paid at Last* does not pick up the water skier. The boy in the water takes the tow handle, signals that he is ready, and the *Paid at Last* sets off again. The lime-green tow rope grows taut and the boy in the water rises perfectly. Miranda's heart is racing. He's got to stay up this time. And the *Paid at Last* must leave the channel—no problem for a small boat like this; it doesn't need depth—and get out of the way.

Miranda focuses the binoculars on the driver.

He is looking upriver, not back at the skier he's towing.

Miranda is watching his arms and hands. She sees him cut back on the throttle.

The tow rope immediately goes slack.

The driver has intentionally dumped his friend in the path of the barge.

She swings the binoculars. The skier is bobbing in the water. Too late, he seems aware that seven hundred thousand gallons of diesel fuel are about to crush him. How terrifying the vast bow of the barge must look. He kicks away the skis and strips off his flotation device so that it won't slow him down.

Upriver, the *Paid at Last* makes a long leisurely circle. It is now safely out of the channel, puttering along Miranda's side of the river. There is no longer time to pick up the boy in the water. Through the magnification of her binoculars, Miranda sees no expression of horror on the driver's face. He seems placid.

He is murdering his friend, thinks Miranda. The barge will suck his friend under and hold him under for a long time.

It's a perfect murder. He'll claim he was stupid and unthinking and he's ever so sorry. And it will go down as a tragic accident.

When she looks back, the water skier is gone.

Miranda prays that he has dived; that he is swimming faster than the fastest fish; that he will pop up safely out of the channel.

But almost certainly he has not dived.

The river is full of currents; it flows down to the sea no matter which direction the tide is going, and with the tide coming in, those two forces roil and whirl. The displacement of all that water by the barge creates a third force, against which his body is as fragile as a leaf. No matter how big a breath he takes, the air will not last long enough. He will be held on the muddy bottom as if by an alligator. Or chopped by the massive propellers of the tug like cabbage in a blender.

Miranda runs down the cliff stairs to join Lander on the dock. "Lanny, he did it on purpose. I saw him. He slowed down on purpose so his friend would fall in the water and be killed."

Lander hates being called Lanny. "That's ridiculous!" she snaps. "Of course he didn't do that. And how could you tell anyway? That's a horrible thing to say. The poor man is thoughtless and inexperienced and now he's going to find himself responsible for a death—but it's an accident, Rimmie!"

Miranda hates being called Rimmie. "Lander, I saw his hand on the throttle. I saw him let the tow rope go slack."

Her sister fixes her with a glare so hostile that Miranda flinches. "This is not a video, Rimmie. This is not television. This is some poor young man drowning and the poor friend who will carry his bad judgment with him forever. Don't make it worse with some vicious exaggeration."

The barge and tug pass by.

Miranda's father is getting into their Zodiac. He will try to find the body. Miranda's mother has come down the stairs to join Miranda and Lander. Incredibly, she is holding a mug of coffee that she has prepared for the boy in the boat. "He'll be in shock," she says. "Signal him, Lander. I've called nine-one-one, they're on the way, but water rescues are slow."

Lander yells at the *Paid at Last*. The driver nods and slowly approaches the Allerdon dock. Miranda finds this as shocking as the murder. The driver should be searching the water, along with the pleasure boats that have cut their engines and are hoping to spot the skier. High up on the tug and barge, the crew stands in horror, looking down, helpless to do a thing. And yet the driver of the boat just tootles up to the nearest dock.

Miranda says, "Where are Henry and Hayden?"

"I sent them home," says her mother. "I don't want them to see what will happen next."

What will happen next is they will find a damaged dead body. Miranda doesn't want to see it either. She wants the swimmer to pop up smiling. "Mom," she says, and she finds breathing hard, as if she too were underwater, "Mom, the driver of that powerboat—he—"

Lander interrupts. "Rimmie. Don't lie. Don't exaggerate. Don't, don't, *don't* repeat that nonsense. Do you want to ruin a second life?"

There is some basis to this ferocity. Miranda in childhood always doubled or tripled any event. If she stubbed her toe, she described a broken ankle and a hospital visit. If her mother slammed on the brakes while driving, Miranda cried out that her ribs were broken and her seat belt torn away. When she returned from playdates, she talked about a sight-seeing helicopter flight instead of her failure to make a helicopter out of a Lego kit.

She hasn't exaggerated (her parents' word) or lied (Lander's) in years, but in Lander's mind, the little sister hasn't grown up and hasn't grown better.

The Coast Guard will come, because it's a water accident. The ambulance will come, because there will be a body. The state police will come. And what will I do? Miranda asks herself. Say nothing? Let it go?

Nobody else saw it. He'll deny it. My sister will say it's my lifelong habit to exaggerate. Everybody will despise me for making a bad situation even worse.

Miranda never wears clothing without pockets because she never goes anywhere without her cell phone. Lander is wrong that this is not a video, because Miranda filmed the *Paid at Last* when it was circling. The driver is very good-looking. It upsets Miranda that she would even notice, under these circumstances.

Lander helps the boy tie up at their narrow dock. Riverine laws do not permit the Allerdons to build a larger dock because the channel here is so close to the shore. One family in their neighborhood has an aluminum dock that is winched up when it is not in use. Some families have waterfront property, but not dock rights. Only one family has land low enough and far enough from the channel for a real dock with a pier.

Lander puts the big striped beach towel around the young man's shoulders and Miranda takes another picture.

Lander and the boy are looking at each other, faces close, and they are both beautiful, with oddly similar profiles. Lander's sympathetic smile looks like the smile of a coconspirator.

Miranda is sickened by this thought.

Lander is right: the little sister still exaggerates in a hideous cruel way. Miranda drops her cell phone back into her pocket.

The boy takes the mug of coffee from Miranda's mother. Maybe coffee is a nice idea for helping someboby in shock, but nevertheless, while his friend is drowning, he's sipping coffee. "It's my fault," he says.

Nobody disagrees.

But Lander and Miranda's mother are thinking that his faulty action led to an accident. Miranda is thinking it is homicide. A murder that takes no time, no effort, no weapon, and will not be found during autopsy.

Behind the barge and tug, young men on Jet Skis have been racing back and forth over the wake, springing up and slapping down on artificial waves, having a great time. They have not seen the tragedy and are shocked when Miranda's father signals from the Zodiac, tells them what happened, asks them to look.

How many deep breaths has Miranda taken since the poor swimmer was swept underwater? A lot.

The boy is young. Maybe twenty. He will not finish college. He will not have a career or get married or have children or go home for Thanksgiving. He will have a funeral and his mother and father will never get over it.

The ambulance comes down their driveway, but a land-bound rescue crew can do nothing.

The Coast Guard patrols on weekends in a little white boat that looks like a tub toy. They try to keep the speed down among powerboats, prevent racing, check permits, monitor safety regulations, fine people for not using flotation devices. The patrol boat will be on its way, but it could be miles from here.

Supposedly the patrol boat also makes sure nobody is doing drug runs. There are plenty of little inlets and tiny winding streams in wide yellow marshes where a boat could drop off illegal substances. But Miranda has never heard of any druggie or criminal being caught along the river, although she has often thought that their own property is perfect for silent, secret comings and goings.

She glances up the bluff. Their little town has a resident state trooper and he is here.

Do I tell him about the tow rope?

But already the image is not clear.

Neighbors gather. There is a whole line of people on the Allerdon bluff. Henry and Hayden either never left in the first place or are back. Jack, the twelve-year-old, and Geoffrey, the fifteen-year-old, want to jump in the water and help with the search, but Miranda's father is not letting them.

Out in the water, the Jet Ski men give a shout. They have the body.

Miranda is amazed. The river does not easily give up its dead. The water carries a body out to sea or lodges it in some sunken tree to become fish food.

On the dock, Lander puts her arm around the boat driver to give him comfort.

"He's alive!" screams the Jet Ski guy.

Lander shrieks with joy. Her face is lit and beautiful.

But the driver is stunned.

Stunned that he has lost his bet? That he has not pulled off a murder?

Or stunned with relief? That his stupidity did not kill his friend after all?

Anyway, Miranda realizes, it can't have been murder because he couldn't have planned it. Who could know the exact schedule of a barge? Even the tug doesn't know. There are too many variables. And what if his friend had learned to ski instantly and was never at risk?

Lander is correct, as always. Miranda is still given to ghastly exaggeration.

At least I didn't say it to anybody else, she thinks.

The ambulance crew orders everybody off the dock, up the stairs and onto the bluff so that they can move a stretcher down the treacherous steep steps. Miranda is used to skittering down, but people trying it the first time usually wish for a lot more to hold on to.

The boy is draped over the lap of one rescuer like clothes

from a dry cleaner, while the other rescuer holds the head out of the water. They insist he is still breathing. If indeed the victim is alive, he must be in agony from jolting over the wake.

The crew maneuvers the body onto the stretcher and the stretcher up the stairs. Not only are the steps very steep, but the only rail is a loose rope at thigh height on one side. It's a little scary.

The state trooper talks to the boat driver, who gives his name and spells it. "Jason Firenza."

Lander's lips move as she silently repeats the name: Jason Firenza. Miranda remembers Lander saying, *That one is mine.*

No, no, Lanny. Don't fall for him. In a month, you'll have your pick of a whole medical school. Don't take a killer!

Miranda wipes away this thought. The guy is not a killer, first because the water skier is alive and second because she is making the whole thing up to start with.

The trooper asks for the skier's name.

"Derry Romaine," says Jason Firenza. "Derry is a student at Wesleyan. Majoring in history. I have to go with him in the ambulance." His bare chest is heaving with emotion. It's a very attractive chest.

"No," says the trooper. "The crew doesn't have room for you."

Barrel is loose again.

Barrel's owners have either slept through all this or

are not in town. More than half the dozen houses here are weekend places and the Nevilles don't make it every weekend. Miranda grabs Barrel's collar, hauls him across the yard, through the shrubbery, over the Nevilles' grass and up to the dog run. Barrel hates his dog run. All those wonderful smells, all this excitement—and he will be in a six-by-thirty-foot cage. He resists.

"I'll do it," says Stu, and she is startled, but relieved that he has crossed the street and come to help. Stu is around Lander's age. He seems neither adult nor child to Miranda; he's always sort of a passerby. He doesn't play catch, he doesn't ever bring a friend when he's going out on the water, he doesn't wrestle with the dog or help at the grill. He does cut through the Allerdon yard a lot—everybody cuts through the yard a lot—but Stu swerves behind bushes if anybody signals him to come on over.

Miranda has never decided whether Stu is painfully shy or just prefers video games to humans.

"What's happening?" asks Stu. His thin reddish-blond hair isn't cut very well. It bumps out over his ears, like little platforms.

"Some poor water skier got dumped in front of the barge."

"Oh, that's what it is. I couldn't see from our house. We might as well live miles into the woods. We really have to get the trees cut down. But my mother loves them. I'd have to do it on the sly."

A normal person would comment on the skier's fate

rather than the height of shade trees. But Stu is probably too busy with his video life to fathom real life.

Stu manages to knee Barrel into the run and latch the gate.

"The good news," Miranda tells Stu, "is that the water skier is alive."

Stu gapes at her. *"Alive?"*

"I know, it seems impossible. But they started an IV before they shut the ambulance door." Miranda heads back to the cottage. Stu doesn't come. There are probably too many real live people around.

The trooper is wrapping up his interview with Jason Firenza. "All right. You can take your boat back to your marina. Then drive to my office. It's at the rear of town hall."

Jason's dark hair ruffles in the wind. He has that need-to-shave look, which definitely works for him. He's holding a Ziploc bag in which he probably has his car keys, cell phone and wallet, to keep these safe and dry while he's on the river. It takes a lot of poise to retrieve all that when your friend is drowning and it's your fault.

"Yes, sir. Thank you," says Jason Firenza.

Lander goes down the cliff stairs with Jason, probably to see him off. But she does not come back up. A few minutes later, the *Paid at Last* is visible, headed downstream. There are two people on board.

Lander has gone with Jason Firenza.

A stab of fear slices Miranda. What if he *is* a murderer?

But the victim—if indeed Derry Romaine is a victim of

anything but his own stupidity—is not dead. There has not been a murder.

Her parents are talking with various neighbors. Geoffrey, Jack and Stu are no longer around. Henry and Hayden have lost interest now that the ambulance is gone and are working on their tree house, a long-term activity involving many failures. Miranda does not want to think about the accident, Jason Firenza or Derry Romaine. She especially does not want to think about Lander, intentionally motoring away with a man who chooses to endanger the lives of his friends.

She goes over to see the latest tree house development.

Henry, the seven-year-old, rushes over. He is the most affectionate little guy. She adores him. If Henry were fifteen, he would be her future. But the fifteen-year-old around here is Geoffrey, who in mind and body is as thick as a post.

"I went on board that powerboat," Henry tells her. "After they took up the stretcher and nobody was on the dock. It's called *Paid at Last*." Henry is very proud of his reading skills. He has been slow to catch on, but now, summer after second grade, he's nailed it. "You know what?" says Henry. "The boat name isn't painted on. It's a magnetic sign you peel off."

How peculiar, thinks Miranda.

"The registration number isn't real either. It's a slap-on sign, too."

"Did you peel them off?" asks Miranda. "What was underneath?"

"I didn't have time. Daddy made me come in. I'm in

big trouble because I could have drowned and the lesson is that the river is very dangerous and little boys should not tell lies."

Miranda is familiar with those lessons.

Henry says, "I bet the real name of the boat is embarrassing." Henry giggles. The family across the road from his house has a boat called *Butter and Sugar*. These are not ingredients of a good dessert, but the names of their Siamese cats.

"I bet you're right," says Miranda, but she doesn't bet that at all. Jason and his friend Derry are probably drug runners. They probably hide their boat by the simple technique of renaming it whenever they're out being criminals.

Miranda starts laughing. Lander is so right. Miranda's need to romanticize a story—so that even a huge story like the near drowning of a water skier under an oil barge has to be bigger, and involve murder, and drug running—is juvenile.

I am hereby an adult, Miranda tells herself. Exaggeration is in my past.

2

She is sitting on a metal chair in a small windowless room, facing a small table with nothing on it. An empty chair sits on the other side. Another empty chair is in the corner. The room was once painted pale green but grime creeps across it like mold. The floor is gray and she cannot tell what it is made of. Concrete? Linoleum? It doesn't feel like America in here. It feels like some grim third-world country; some building that should have been demolished but is still used.

She cannot stop shivering. She is a quivering blob. She is Jell-O.

She does not approve of Jell-O. It has artificial coloring and too much sugar. There is no nutritional point to Jell-O. A person should consume only those foods that come directly from the earth.

It is easier to think about food than about her situation.

Every now and then the police come in, occupy the chairs and talk to her again.

She knows they are talking to her but she cannot go there. The questions are so terrible.

She has a plan. She will stand up and walk out and end this.

But although there is a door in the room, there is no way out.

They keep telling her that the way out is to talk to them but her own terrible answers bang around her skull. I am a good person, she tells herself. My goal is to help humanity. That is my reason for living. They're making up the part about the dead body. There was no one there! I did not kill anybody!

The police try a tough approach, a friendly approach and the silent treatment.

If she can stay firm against them, they have to give up. They can keep her here only a certain number of hours, right? And then they have to charge her. But she has done nothing, absolutely nothing, so there is no charge they can bring, and she will leave, and it will be over.

An image of herself shooting that gun comes back into her mind. She smells the marsh, hears the birds, feels the damp hot wind. The gun is heavier in her hand than she expects. He is standing next to her, coaxing, guiding. They are both laughing. She can hear their laughter. She is in love with his laugh.

She is in love with everything. He fills her soul as if she were just clothing before; just fabric on a hanger. She is richer because he is here; because he wants her company.

They are standing in the woods and she has that gun in her hand. "Go on, do it," he breathes. "It's fun. You're going to love the power of it."

So she shoots. And it is fun.

He puts the gun away. He gives her an air kiss and says he'll be back in a minute. Just checking on something.

She does not ask him what there can be to check on in a little woods off a little creek by a little marsh. She is completely happy to stand and wait, because she will have the joy of watching him return.

But he does not return.

Somehow the state police are there instead. Somehow she is sitting in a jail.

Her teeth are chattering. *I have done nothing but go out on a date,* she tells herself. *And on this date, have I murdered somebody?*

If it is true, her life is over.

She tries to worry about the dead person, whose life really is over.

They suggest that she make a phone call.

But to whom?

She knows kids in law school. But no real lawyers. She could call her parents. But she is hoping that this will end before her parents even realize there is a beginning.

She is weeping again. She does not approve of tears.

Tears are for some other generation. Women need to be in control. She cannot dissolve, especially not now.

They set a box of tissues in front of her. Cheap stuff. No double layers. No aloe, no scent.

They set her cell phone in front of her.

She knows it's hers because of the frosted mint-green bumper. She yearns to hold its slim rectangular comfort in the palm of her hand. She can tap her father's cell phone number. Turn this all over to him.

And then *his* life will be over, his brilliant daughter now the source of shame and horror.

SATURDAY AFTERNOON

Hours have passed since the ambulance and the state troopers left, and the neighbors have all gone home.

Miranda is on the riding mower. The lawn is a great green square entirely wrapped by trees. She cannot see through the trees because their trunks are deep in azalea, mountain laurel and rhododendron. A driver on the narrow country lane cannot see through the trees either, and would never know there is a house or a river right here.

She loves mowing; she loves the scent of cut grass. It's work without actually working, because the mower does everything but steer. This afternoon her mind is too free. She cannot think of anything but the half-dead skier and her half-sure murder theory.

The Allerdons' driveway cuts through the trees and slopes

down the hill to the house. Miranda is startled to see Lander walking down the drive. Where has Lander come from?

Jason, so he tells the trooper, keeps his boat at Two Willows Marina. Two Willows is on the west bank and downstream a few miles. The Allerdon cottage is on the east bank. So after they leave the *Paid at Last* at Two Willows, Jason must bring Lander home in his car—no short drive, because few bridges cross the Connecticut. But why drop her on the road? Why not bring her to the house? What have the two of them been doing all this time? Have they been at the hospital with Derry Romaine? Is Derry Romaine going to survive?

Lander is walking slowly, and this too is odd, because Lander does not amble through life. She waves to Miranda, and walks on.

Miranda has quite a bit more grass to cut. She wants to go inside and hear everything, but Lander discusses big things like politics, art class and European travel. She does not discuss her life. If Miranda weren't a Facebook friend, she'd know approximately nothing about her big sister. And given Lander's disgust—horror, even—over Miranda's tow rope description, Lander will not be chatty about Jason Firenza and Derry Romaine.

Geoffrey also comes down the lane.

"What's up?" yells Miranda over the engine racket. "No bushes for you today?"

Geoffrey grins, and she is so surprised by facial action on a person she thinks of as blank that she grins back. "I heard the mower," shouts Geoffrey. "I was hoping for an update."

Courtesy requires her to turn off the mower. But the mower is hard to start and she doesn't want to struggle with it a second time. "I don't have one," she yells. "You know Lanny. She just walked right by without telling me anything. I'll go inside and interrogate her after a while." Miranda gazes at the remaining stretch of grass and Geoffrey gets the hint. He walks down the grass and around the cottage to the river's edge.

It's such a waste. Miranda is so ready to have a boy in her life and here's Geoffrey—same age, same grade although different school system—walking at least twice a day through her yard, and she can't work up a molecule of interest in him.

It's another half hour before Miranda drives the big mower into the shed and padlocks the door. There is little crime here, and half the time they forget to lock the house, but somehow the shed seems vulnerable and they usually remember to lock that.

Her parents and Lander are on the screened porch, where Miranda gratefully accepts a tall glass of sparkling water from her mother. She is parched. She starts in on Lander. "So did you go with him to the police? What did they say? Is everything all right? Will they charge him with anything? How is Derry Romaine? Has he regained consciousness? What hospital is he in?"

She knows from their posture that her parents have none of these answers. But Lander's usual sharp exclusionary retort does not come. Lander smiles. It's a slow, warm-honey smile. Rigid, disciplined, careful Lander has stars in her eyes.

Miranda's sister has a crush on a frustrated murderer?

Miranda doesn't think Lander has ever really been in love. In high school Lander traveled in a smart, exciting crowd and yet she had nothing resembling a date that Miranda ever knew of. Well, proms. Big dances. But they went in a group. In college, as far as Lander's Twitter and Facebook represent it, her social life was similar. Groups, crowds, bunches, buddies. Nobody special.

What is special about Jason Firenza? Is it that thing called chemistry, as if love is nothing but the mixing of molecules?

"Two Willows is a charming marina," says Lander. "I've never been there before. It has this darling little park, with picnic tables and some of those pastel-painted wooden lounge chairs. They've strung a big striped sunshade between two maple trees and you hang out there and have a wonderful view of the river."

Lander does not use words like "darling" or "charming." And nobody could have a more wonderful view than the Allerdons have already.

Did you peel away the magnetic strip that covers the real name of that boat? Miranda wants to ask. *And is Jason a drug runner?*

But her sister's happiness is as visible as if Lander has dyed her hair maroon or put on hip boots.

Miranda loves lots of people. She has not been blessed with love for a boy. She's had crushes on classmates and celebrities. Once a boy had a crush on Miranda and it was exciting but awful, because she felt nothing toward him. What's the matter with her? Is she going to have such high standards that she'll never even find a boy?

On the other hand, standards can fall. Perfect Lander is now mad about very imperfect Jason.

Miranda tells herself that her eyes deceived her when that tow rope went slack. "What are you and Jason Firenza doing tomorrow?" she asks brightly, because a sister dizzy with love has plans for tomorrow.

Miranda knows she has not set aside the idea of Jason Firenza as homicidal or she wouldn't need to tack on his last name. The name Jason is warm, friendly, ordinary. It's a popular name. In fact, J is a popular name-starter. The boys in Miranda's school are named Jack and Jaxon, Jaden and Joshua and Jett.

Lander's sharp eyes are unfocused. Her lips are smiling. "Right now he's checking on Derry, and then he and I are going out for dinner."

Lander has her cell phone in her hand. They all do. Miranda's father is undoubtedly checking emails from work. Her mother is probably looking at Pinterest, because although she is not crafty, she adores the idea of craft. Just as she has never cooked anything from those TV shows that demonstrate cooking, but happily watches them on the Food Network.

Lander is texting. Probably Jason. Or else her best friend, Willow, updating her on the joys of Jason.

For no particular reason, Miranda people-searches Jason

Firenza. In the entire United States there are only fourteen people with that last name and also a *J* first name. None of these is Jason.

She narrows the search to Connecticut. No Firenza at all.

Their parents have not heard Miranda's claim that Jason Firenza intentionally dropped his friend in harm's way, but they certainly know the man is careless, has no judgment and is not to be trusted on the water. Yet their beloved daughter spends half a day with him and now the evening? Their father says, "Lanny, I'm not happy with this. He may be a fine person, but he's not fine on the river."

Lander is still beaming. "I'll teach him. Don't worry, Dad."

Miranda shivers. Jason Firenza almost killed somebody a few hours ago. Shouldn't Jason be camped at Derry's bedside? Or picking Derry's parents up at the airport? Talking with doctors? What's up with all the happy smiling?

Out loud, Miranda says, "What restaurant?"

Lander is not that fond of restaurants. She accuses them of slow service, which Lander feels should be a crime. Lander says that when she is a successful surgeon, she will employ a cook. She will eat extremely well at home, and be known for her dinner parties.

Lander turns to Miranda, her smile wide and joyful, and the smile showers Miranda with sisterly love, even though that's not what it is. It's love for Jason Firenza, spilling over. But to have Lander beam at her like that—to have Lander share anything, even a smile!—Miranda softens.

"He'll meet me at the dock," says Lander. "We're going to canoe in the moonlight."

The Allerdons are often on the river in the evening. No matter how dark the night, the river reflects the slightest sparkle of star and moon. It will be romantic.

"What will you wear?" Miranda asks.

Lander always looks terrific, but she doesn't care much about clothing. She's so tall and slim and elegant that anything looks good. She sticks with classic styles, to cut down on the amount of shopping she has to do.

Miranda almost drops her water glass when Lander asks, sounding needy, "Do you think maybe the yellow cutoffs? And could I borrow that white shirt of yours, the one with the lace sides?"

They can't trade clothing; their heights are too different. But that particular shirt is a medium, and Miranda uses it as a light summer jacket. It will probably fit her sister perfectly. In fact, she is willing to bet that Lander has tried it on previously, or even taken it previously, and already knows that it will be perfect.

"Sure," says Miranda. "Let's go see what scarf would look right."

Their bedrooms are small identical cubes on the south side of the cottage. They share a very tight bathroom, which is also the powder room for guests. It has no countertop at all, and the shower has no shelf, so the sisters have little—or in Miranda's case, large—wire totes in which they bring all products and necessities in and out of the bathroom.

They even have to hang their towels and washcloths in their rooms, because the bathroom has space for exactly one hand towel, and that is for guests.

In Miranda's room the two of them take up all floor space. Miranda removes the white shirt from the hanger, gives it to her sister and sits cross-legged on the bed to give Lander room to change.

Lander has a beautiful body. Miranda, so much shorter, yearns for height. The shirt is so much better on Lander than on Miranda that she wards off a stab of jealousy.

She pictures Jason in a canoe and is vaguely puzzled. Is this canoe also at Two Willows? Is Jason Firenza going to paddle two miles upstream before the date even begins? He has a nice muscular body, but he seems more like a power-boat kind of guy. Canoes are work.

"Lanny," she says softly.

"Rimmie, you know I don't like that nickname any more than you like your nickname."

"I'm sorry," she corrects herself. "Lander." Lander will be gone for good in a month. What if Miranda's next statement drives them apart, and they never come together, and they are never close, and she might as well not even have a sister? Miranda braces herself. "Lander, it's frightening. What happened on the river. Maybe he was just careless, but it looked so much worse. And Henry says that—"

Lander neither looks at Miranda nor speaks. She simply drifts out of the room, goes into her own and shuts the door.

3

The police have moved her into a cell.

The walls are cement block, heavily painted so that the pitted surface is not so rough.

There are bars.

Her eyes flicker open for a moment, and then she squeezes them shut.

The jail is noisy. Prisoners curse, moan, mutter and sob. She cannot see the men and women making these sounds. She is horrified by the word "prisoner." *How can she be one?*

The air conditioning is intense. She shivers.

She is sitting on a metal shelf. A few inches away, the toilet stinks.

Her shorts are knee length. When she sits, the shorts ride up, and the backs of her legs are naked against this metal bench. What bacteria are crawling around, seeping into her? What roaches and insects will she spot if she opens her eyes?

Her sneakers rest on a floor that looks clean, and yet seems layered with filth, as if urine has sunk into the concrete and been painted over.

Her sneakers are fashionable. The soles are orange, the canvas lavender with a scroll of silver and orange. The laces are silver, but a policewoman pulls the laces out and keeps them. Her socks are footies: thin white cotton with a little purple trimming. They do not keep her feet warm. The colors of her shoes and socks seem irrational; seem hideous.

She wants to vomit.

She wants the lights to dim. Bulbs glare at her. Even with her eyes closed, the light gives her a headache.

She cannot remember being without her cell phone. At night, at home, she does not even put her phone on the bedside table, but nestles it next to her pillow. She sleeps around it, like a partner, never letting it fall to the floor. She prefers clothing where she can tuck her phone into a pocket. Otherwise, she has a tiny case that can snap on a belt or hang on a thin strap. Sometimes she resorts to a purse, although there's something cluttered and annoying about handbags that she despises.

They ask about his phone. They ask over and over. She could answer, but she doesn't.

She soothes herself with sweet safe memory.

Last Saturday morning, six days ago, when the state

trooper says that Jason Firenza can go, she follows him down the steps from her yard to the dock, planning to say some comforting good-bye. Offer some hopeful thought. But he takes her hand and looks at her almost with fear.

"Would you come with me?" he asks. "Please? This whole thing is so . . ." He searches for the right word. She is touched that he is not tossing out some swearword, but is trying to find the adjective that fits this nightmare.

She has always wanted to be a physician; to cure by cutting or prescribing. Standing there on the narrow dock, holding his hand, she wants to be a nurse or a mother to him; to cure by kindness and caring.

Poor Jason doesn't want to be alone with his fears. She will keep him company; ward off his guilt. They are together for hours, dealing with the marina, trying to get into the hospital to see Derry. But Derry is in surgery. By the time Jason drops her at the cottage, she is in love.

Jason asks her out.

Her mouth is dry and her heart rushing at the thought of an actual date. Dates are rare in her world. The college men she knows would rather deal with cancer than commitment. The armor of the college man is the group.

She is dizzy with wanting to be at Jason's side.

Dizzy because this afternoon he needs her to protect himself from the pain of Derry's accident, but tonight— this will be solely for the pleasure of her company.

They don't take the canoe after all. She steps again into the *Paid at Last*. When she steals a glance at Jason, she blushes. They tie up at a different marina. He suggests that she could powder her nose in the marina office. It's so sweet that his first thought is her comfort; that he would phrase it in such an old-fashioned way.

When she comes out, he is waiting for her, smiling. It's a sad smile, full of his burden: Derry's injuries.

They walk through a parking lot for cars, and then a parking lot filled with boats for sale, across an acre of grass in need of mowing and finally over the gravel parking lot of a riverbank restaurant.

She has eaten here many times. Brightly painted tables are scattered on the deck, porch and grass. There is seating inside, for bad weather or when the insects are intolerable. When her family eats here, motoring over in their Zodiac, they eat out on the pier, sitting on narrow wooden benches, their table a piece of plywood that folds out like a gate. They love dining fifty feet out in the river.

She and Jason order. The waiter leaves. The two of them talk. Dinner arrives quickly. Or else time flies in his presence.

She is amazed by the depth of her crush on him. It's all she can do to breathe, never mind chew.

He smiles at her—oh, but he has a lovely smile!—and waves his phone. He has to take this call, he apologizes, and he walks out of hearing range. She is mildly surprised. People her parents' age might search for a private spot, but she and her friends do not care what they say in front of each other.

When he returns, he is sliding his phone into his shirt pocket. She knows her phones and is astonished. It's not a smartphone. It is a prepaid, disposable phone. It has no apps. He cannot check Facebook. He cannot play games or read.

Nobody on a college campus has anything less than the best phone he can afford. Jason has a lot of money; it's clear from the shoes he wears; the sunglasses; their dinner out.

But his phone is a cheap throwaway. Perhaps he is also too mature for games and social media. She thinks of poor Stu, across the street, with whom she has had one dull, pitiful dinner. Stu lives for video games. At that restaurant, Stu ate with his fork in one hand and his cell in the other. Lander came in third, after food and phone. Which does not matter at all, because Stu is so useless she doesn't even rank him.

But this time? With this man? Lander aches to be first on Jason's list.

He returns from his phone call, bends over her, sweeps her hair from her face. She wants to know a thousand things about him. She wants to kiss.

But in fact, this is a week-old memory. In fact, she is in a cell, surrounded by invisible swearing prisoners, trembling in short sleeves because the air conditioning feels as if it's set at sixty degrees.

The police insist that drugs are stashed in that boat of his. Not a little bit of weed, but a serious package of cocaine.

She cannot swallow. Saliva builds in her mouth, horror in her heart.

A person dealing drugs uses a disposable phone. Is that what he is? A dealer?

Is that what he's done? Left her with that package?

He didn't mean to, she tells herself. *He meant to come back. He's afraid of the police. It isn't his drug package! He's been forced to deliver it! He's a good person.*

But she knows nothing of this man she adores. Do her teeth chatter because of the cold or because she spends six days with a man and learns nothing—nothing at all—about him?

She thinks of her tendency to scorn her little sister, who exaggerates. She is now the opposite: a person of science—who nevertheless does not bother with a single fact once she is in love.

He's a good person, she repeats in her heart. And what am I? A good person? Or a killer?

Please, please, God, don't let me be a killer. Please don't let this happen to me. Get me out of here.

She is on her knees now, in front of the metal toilet that has no seat. She is retching so hard the vomit gets in her hair. Her hands have vomit on them.

When the last awful sour slime leaves her throat, when she has spit out all that she can, she cannot get up.

She is aware of somebody lifting her at the waist; standing her on her feet; handing her water in a plastic cup so cheap that if she holds it tightly she will squash it. She manages to swallow some, manages to whisper, "Thank you."

She says, "I have to wash my hands and face. I have to wash my hair."

She is given a wet paper towel, the brown kind, which dissolves in her hand. The vomit dries in her hair.

"It's so cold. Can I have a blanket?"

They give her a square of fleece, more of a shawl than a blanket. She huddles in it. It is not clean.

Neither are her thoughts.

FRIDAY MORNING

Miranda's summer days are long and slow.

Such a pleasure to do nothing after a crushingly hard school year.

Miranda is given to short-lived passions. This year, in music, she drops violin and takes up bass clarinet, which she played for a while in elementary school, so that she can now join marching band. The hours of rehearsal required for marching band and the Saturday games force her to drop tennis, Spanish club and horseback riding. She lasts through the football season in marching band, but does not continue through the winter with concert band. She means to return to violin, but ends up in sketching class and competing in math tournaments. She fails to make the softball team and takes up clogging.

Lander is disgusted. Show discipline! she snaps. Don't give up so easily. Choose one thing. Work hard. Excel.

Miranda is never interested in one thing. She is always interested in a hundred. She does not mind doing poorly in anything as long as she gets to try it all.

This summer, while she is doing nothing, her high school friends commit to fascinating volunteer work, exciting paid work, demanding summer camps and challenging study abroad. Friends who normally visit the cottage for a week, a weekend or a day don't show up. They are too busy.

But Miranda Allerdon is lazy and loving it.

Early Friday morning, six days after the barge disaster, another barge is on the river, coming downstream and riding high because it's empty. It is pushed by the tug *Susan and Jane*. For once, Miranda does not race outside to wave. It's too early. She's too comfy on the chaise lounge. But it does remind her of that people search for Jason Firenza.

Having failed to find a Jason Firenza, she decides to find out more about Derry Romaine. Using her iPad is satisfying. She feels less lazy, even though the search engine is doing the work.

There is exactly one Derry Romaine in America and his first name is Derek, not Derry. He is decades older than the Derry Romaine who nearly drowned.

Miranda tries to think of a credible reason for two young men who clearly exist, breathe and own a boat to have names that don't exist.

Over breakfast—Henry and Hayden show up; really, do

their parents ever do any parenting? Is food ever served? Does conversation ever take place?—Miranda's mother says to Lander, "Are you and Jason going somewhere today?"

Their mother has planned this question carefully. It must not be too invasive. It must show interest, but not start conflict. Her parents always tiptoe around Lander. Well, so do I, thinks Miranda. We don't want to be on her hit list.

"Yes," says Lander, smiling. Her vision of Jason is so wonderful she can't sit. She gets up and dances.

Out the window, Miranda sees Geoffrey approaching the dock stairs. Since Miranda goes to school in West Hartford, and Geoffrey goes to school here, she does not know anything about his high school life or his friends. He does swim a lot but today he doesn't descend the stairs and slide into the water. He lifts one of the big heavy wooden lawn chairs, moves it closer to the steps and sits down heavily. Is he going to fish off the bluff instead of the dock? Is he taking in the view? Does Miranda care?

Lander dances on. Miranda tries to imagine herself dancing at the vision of Geoffrey in her life. It doesn't play. "How is Derry Romaine doing?" she asks Lander. "Do we have news about him yet?"

"Well, of course, Jason visits him constantly. He's sitting up and they're making him walk around, but he's dazed from medication and isn't talking much. They've done one surgery and another is scheduled. Jason is so thankful that Derry is probably going to be okay."

Miranda wonders about this. *Is* Jason Firenza thankful?

Lander is certainly spending a lot of time with Jason. Jason himself does not appear; Lander goes to meet him. Once she kayaks across the river. Twice she takes the Zodiac.

It's creepy. People throng to the cottage. They can't get enough of the porch, the view, the dock. Why does Jason never even show up, let alone hang out?

Even now Stu is carrying his inflatable orange kayak over to the stairs. It's the only kayak Miranda has ever seen with a cup holder. He's got the foot pump and the seat under his other arm and a daypack over his back.

Stu and Geoffrey nod to each other, but do not speak. They are a remarkable contrast: Stu is as thin as a plastic fork and Geoffrey as solid as a baseball bat.

Miranda believes that Geoffrey will grow into a pretty normal decent guy; he just needs time and maybe fewer pounds. But Stu is twenty-three and probably already is what he's going to be. Not much.

One weekend, Stu asks Lander out, and either she's extremely bored that day or believes Stu has possibilities. It's a short date. Lander comes home rolling her eyes. "What?" Miranda asks. "Stu," replies her sister. "We're talking serious limitations. He's dropped out of three colleges. Thinks he's going to develop the world's best video game, but all he does is play other people's games. I despise men who don't make an effort."

Miranda is distracted by the word "men," because she thinks of Stu as a boy.

Lander can be brusque with people who don't measure up. Miranda imagines Lander saying to Stu, *This won't work. I associate only with the top one half of one percent.* But Stu calls Lander at least two more times, hoping for a second chance. He has the wrong lady. Lander is one tough judge.

Their father interrupts Lander's dancing. "So tell us more about Jason. He must be a very interesting young man."

Normally, Lander looks like a model in a *New York Times Magazine:* thin and intensely sulky, as if her best friend just died. Why this should sell clothing is a mystery to Miranda. If the clothing makes you feel that way, don't put it on.

Lander giggles at the mention of Jason. The family is scooped up like ice cream at the sight of Lander giggling. They let the interrogation slide. Lander dances.

Miranda has sworn off exaggeration, but she has not sworn off curiosity.

Derry Romaine is supposed to be a student at Wesleyan. Perhaps he is. But his name doesn't show up in Connecticut. Shouldn't his name exist somewhere else in the nation, then? His parents' house? His orphanage?

Why doesn't Lander tell them anything about Jason? Why doesn't Jason come to the house, like a normal person?

Through Lander, Miranda knows quite a few undergrads or recent graduates of Wesleyan. Perhaps Jason Firenza also goes there, or went there, or visits. She could forward the headshot of Jason Firenza to Lander's Wesleyan friends and ask if they recognize him or if they know Derry Romaine. But if they do know Jason, they'll text him to ask what's up, and Jason will ask Lander, and Lander will come home and kill Miranda.

As far as she can tell, no media covers the story of the near drowning under the barge, probably because it's not a story; for it to be newsworthy, the drowning has to end in drowning.

She tries to find a boat registry online and get information about the *Paid at Last*. But although she can find regulations about boats, she cannot find lists. She wonders whether Jason has gone back to talk to the police again. Has the Coast Guard talked to the tug captain? What did the *Janet Anne*'s captain put in his report? Did Jason produce his Safe Boating Certificate and his picture ID for the police?

It's been several days, but the Coast Guard—understaffed, overworked—is probably not rushing on a situation that's working out all right in the end. As for the police, a water incident is not under their purview; they just happened to be there as part of the rescue response. It may be that they have already forgotten Jason Firenza.

Miranda's father sets out for the office. He takes his vacation in half days so he can doze and savor breakfast on the river. Setting out at eleven or twelve also means he will have no traffic going into Hartford. Since it's Friday, though, his drive back down here will be in heavy traffic.

As soon as his car is out of sight, Lander says casually that she plans to spend the whole day with Jason. Maybe the night. Nobody is to worry.

Miranda's mother does not want Lander spending the night with anybody, least of all this person who cannot be bothered even to come to the house. Who drops her daughter off in the road, or at the dock! It's insulting and it's weird.

But their mother has not interfered with Lander's choices in a long time. Miranda decides that when she is a parent, she will be strict. On the other hand, Lander certainly has turned out impressively. Maybe her parents are doing the right thing.

And this morning Lander is absolutely beautiful.

She is wearing white shorts that she may actually have ironed, because they have that crisp-edged look that does not come from a dryer. They are quite long, stopping just above her knees. She has chosen a turquoise shirt, on which she buttons only two buttons. Her flat tummy shows above the waist of her shorts.

Normally on the water they wear old cheap sneakers that can get wet and who cares. But for Jason, Lander wears lovely expensive sneakers in great colors. Her tote bag is a giveaway from a makeup counter. Although Lander rarely wears makeup, she loves buying it. In this tote, she will have the shoes she is going to wear when they ditch the boat. Because of the turquoise shirt, Miranda is guessing that Lander is taking her favorite sandals, on which bright-blue stones glitter. Lander has beautiful feet.

Lander has tied her long sleek hair up with a thin turquoise ribbon. At one and the same time, she looks about ten years old and about twenty-five.

Miranda utters a quick prayer that Jason is a good person after all, or at least can grow into being a good person.

The green towline image enters her mind again.

Jason is not a good person.

She wants to warn her sister again—to cry out, *He's bad news! Stay away from him!*

But her sister is so happy.

And their mother, seeing this happiness, also lets it go. Lander's happiness is worth a lot to her.

Miranda follows Lander off the porch and down the steps and onto the grass. "Lander," she says softly.

Her sister turns. She is glowing.

Miranda whispers, "Be careful, okay?"

"Oh, Rimmie," says her sister indulgently, affectionately. This is so rare that tears spring to Miranda's eyes. "I'm fine. He's fine. Everything's fine."

Lander runs lightly down the narrow steps. Her cell phone rings. In a voice of sparkle and music, she sings out, "I'm ready. I'm on the dock, Jason."

Henry and Hayden are playing on the screened porch as if they live here. They have a playroom larger than Miranda's cottage, thigh-high with toys, but are entranced by her old Weebles and a tow truck that makes noise when it backs up.

Miranda's mother volunteers Friday afternoons at the urgent care clinic. Today she is first having lunch with a friend. She departs. Miranda is in the mood for solitude and tells Henry and Hayden to go home.

"We can't," says Henry, the older, responsible one. "Mommy and Daddy went shopping."

Miranda stares at him.

"Well, we're over here," Henry points out. "We're fine."

Mr. and Mrs. Warren have not asked if this is fine with Miranda. It is not the first time this has happened.

It occurs to Miranda that her own parents are pretty dismissive of their younger daughter. Of course she is fifteen. But the fact is, they too have left. Lander is off with a person who doesn't exist and five male people not related to Miranda are using her dock, her kitchen and her bathroom.

Stu has paddled away.

Jack is now fishing off the little dock.

Geoffrey is swimming. Miranda would not swim where somebody is casting a line with a hook, but Geoffrey is not the brightest star in the sky.

"Let's play badminton!" says Henry.

Badminton with little short guys who always miss the birdie is no fun, plus it would be very sweaty on a day like this. "No."

"Croquet, then!" begs Henry.

But since Henry and Hayden do nothing except whack their balls into the bushes, and they all have to crawl around feeling for the balls under the thick green leaves, and sometimes the leaves are poison ivy, Miranda refuses croquet too.

She would like to go for a run. The path along the road is entirely in the shade, huge green trees forming an arch over the pavement. Track is one of Miranda's short-lived interests. It turns out that running is fun only if she chooses the pace. Running is not fun when it is a competition. And she can't run at all with Henry and Hayden, whose legs are too short.

"Let's take Barrel for a walk," she says resignedly, and the boys whoop with joy. It's one of their pluses, that they are always enthusiastic.

Barrel knows they're coming for him.

He goes wild inside his run, his lovely long-haired tail whipping around. He doesn't bark. Barrel is the best kind of mutt: he came out perfectly and probably should be a breed of his own.

There is rarely traffic because the road doesn't go anywhere and few people live on it. But they stay on the path, single file, Barrel first. The little boys stop when Barrel does, lifting their legs, too, sniffing the weeds and hooting with laughter.

Miranda forgets her irritation. The wind is fresh and sweet. She lives in a beautiful place, is out with a beautiful dog and loved by crazy little boys.

If Jason Firenza is a problem, he's Lander's problem.

Miranda's best friend, Candy, texts. Candy is in West

Hartford, where Miranda really lives and goes to school, and Candy has not visited once this summer because she's a full-time junior counselor at Camp Courant, the city's free day camp.

Miranda sends Candy a short video of Henry and Hayden being dogs next to a hydrant. Candy responds with a video of herself using a peashooter made of PVC pipe parts. She's spitting miniature marshmallows on nearby campers, who are demanding marshmallow guns of their own.

Miranda requests two marshmallow shooters for herself. Then she texts her mother, who will stop off at the grocery on her way home. Get miniature marshmallows.

Jack will be up for this. She and Henry versus Jack and Hayden, in a marshmallow war. Or should she make an effort with the only boy her own age, and coax Geoffrey to join in?

It sounds very committed, to ask a boy her own age. Miranda realizes with a disturbing jolt that she is slightly afraid of boys her own age. Little boys are comfy. The right boys are risky.

But since Geoffrey is not the right boy, she can dismiss this unpleasant insight and continue to walk dogs and little guys. Besides, look what happens when Lander goes out exactly one time with a neighborhood boy—he's still around and it's still awkward. Better to ignore the boy next door.

4

Sooner or later, she will have to go to the bathroom.

It's not a phrase that works in jail. She won't "go" any-where. There is no separate room and there is no bath. The metal toilet doesn't have a seat. She cannot sit on that foul rim. She has thrown up on that, and who knows what any-body has done before that? The policewoman, wearing dis-posable gloves, runs a wad of wet paper towel around the rim, but doesn't scrub. There are no bleach wipes.

Hours pass.

She knows because a woman in another cell keeps beg-ging to be told the time. The woman is sure that any minute now, somebody will bail her out.

Bail. That's when your family raises money and the

judge lets you go home. Then it all gets sorted out without you being there.

She thinks of her West Hartford home. She has a separate bathroom, with her own towels. A soft bed, with her own sheets. In the sprawling kitchen, the refrigerator, pantry and freezer are full of food bought specifically to please her. There are televisions. Music. Sofas. Soft drinks.

Bail.

The idea of being released shortly calms her.

She is able to consider questions the police ask about Jason.

Where does he live? they want to know.

She and Jason spend delicious, lovely, funny days together. They laugh, kiss, embrace. They talk of guilt and God. They discuss accidents of nature and the nature of stupidity. They gaze on sunsets and each other. They do not need autobiographies. They have love.

But the fact is, she does not know where Jason lives. He is fascinated by where *she* lives. He estimates that the cottage sits on an acre. She tells him it's an acre and a half. It's hard to gauge because of all the trees.

When she brings friends to the cottage, they invariably check Zillow to find out its worth. Riverfront is valuable, but the shabby cottage is not. The kind of person who could afford the land would bulldoze their beloved little place to build a mansion. Her father says they are the last people who will ever live here.

Where does he go to college? the police ask.

The state of Connecticut is small. She has friends on almost every campus, and has visited Wesleyan, Trinity and the University of Connecticut; Yale, Conn College and the University of Hartford. She and Jason compare parties on those campuses. She speaks from hearsay. She is not a party person. Her friends love the buzzy diminished control that comes from drink and weed, but nothing is interesting to Lander if she cannot run the situation.

She is not running this.

I don't know where he goes to college, she thinks, and there is something profoundly horrible about this. She knows nothing about the man she loves.

They bring her out of the cell again. Cuffed.

This cannot be her life. She cannot be a person under suspicion of *murder*.

They pass a cell with several female prisoners. The women seem to reach for her, arms flapping like insect legs, as if they might crawl onto her and use her flesh for their escape route. She is grateful that the police realize she is not the kind of person who should share space with such scary women.

The hall turns a corner, and at the end of this hall is an exit door, which someone opens from the other side, and now they are away from the cells and in a regular corridor. The acrid smell of her vomit and other people's toilets is gone.

There is a door labeled RESTROOM.

She stops walking.

She does not normally ask permission to do things. That

is simply not on her chart. But this is like kindergarten. She has to have permission to use this bathroom. She whispers to the hallway, because she cannot look at the policewoman leading her by the arm. If she meets her eyes, this is going to get real. She cannot let it get real. She whispers to the hallway instead. "May I use the ladies' room?"

"There was a toilet in the cell."

"I can't use that." This is a fact, and she feels the policewoman should understand.

And the woman does. She unlocks the restroom door. She unlocks the handcuffs. She cuffs Lander to a large metal wall handle, too solid for hanging a towel. It's for attaching a prisoner.

There is a seat on the toilet, but it's up, since it was last used by a guy, and the guy—or many guys—had lousy aim. The thought of touching that seat, lowering it, sitting there brings her to tears yet again. She despises tears. Tears are for the weak.

But she is bursting. The policewoman stands in the door, watching.

She pretends this *is* kindergarten, and this is her kindergarten teacher, being a warm, fussy sweet help. Mrs. McCune was her kindergarten teacher. Mrs. McCune loved to draw on the whiteboard with colored markers, and she drew a scene for every season, and all the children were in awe.

This gets her through the use of the toilet, and there is a sink, although the soap dispenser is empty; at least her hand is rinsed. There is no mirror, which is probably a good thing.

And now they are back in the little room with the two chairs and the little table. Her left wrist is fastened to her chair. It's medieval. It's wrong. She will become an attorney instead of a physician and go after police brutality.

The policewoman asks questions softly and kindly, as if she is Mrs. McCune.

There's a man here too, but apparently not a policeman, because he is not in uniform nor is he armed. He wears a suit, and leans on the wall casually, as if part of some other event.

"Come on, honey," says the policewoman. "You were nice and chatty when we found you on the boat. Just start up again. You're in real trouble and you're making it worse. Protecting your boyfriend is not helping you."

If he's her boyfriend, why isn't he here? *Is* she protecting him? From what? What does she think Jason has done?

But that's the whole problem. She can't figure out what either of them has done.

She sees herself on the boat with Jason.

Although the sisters have grown up with a summer cottage on a river, and often go out in boats, neither is a boat person. In truth, the water is boring. There's only so much excitement a person can have driving up and down a river. Fishing is for ten-year-olds. Swimming and water-skiing are fine two or three times a summer.

But Jason comes for her by water, dates her by water, kisses her by water. This Friday morning, in the little woods and the deep marsh, they finished target shooting and he told her what a fine huntress she will make, how proud he is—and then, where did he go?

And the police. Where did they come from? Do they routinely patrol the little swamp? Was it an accident that they stumbled on her? No. They walked right up, as if they had been told she was there. Yet only Jason knew Lander's location at that minute.

Did Jason call the police?

She cannot accept this. He loves her! He doesn't want her in trouble.

Again the policewoman asks for Jason's phone number.

She doesn't have it. Each time they part, he tells her when and where they will meet next. *You kayak over to Two Willows Marina at noon, and I'll be there.* It's so romantic.

She doesn't know guys who bother with sweet, gentle flirting and funny private jokes. The guys she knows get to the point: let's hook up.

Jason is constantly texting when they are together.

It does not bother her. Certainly she never stops using her phone. But he does not text her and he does not give her his cell phone number.

She is hurt. She wants to be in touch with him every waking minute. When she is not at his side, she is thinking of things she'd like to text. She does text a few friends; she does post a few pictures; but next to Jason, the world and all her acquaintances pale.

Jason's phone lives in his hand, and sometimes driving

the boat is tricky because he needs two hands, and then he holds the phone in his teeth.

Perhaps this was what Miranda misunderstood when Derry Romaine was in trouble in the river—Jason was simply on the phone and distracted. For sure, Miranda did not see Jason intentionally drop Derry in the water. Jason and Derry are dear friends. Jason visits Derry daily at the hospital. Derry is doing better, he tells her. No, Derry's parents haven't come. Jason doesn't know anything about Derry's parents. Doesn't know how to reach them. The hospital is probably doing that.

"What kind of car does Jason drive?" ask the police.

They have driven a few times. One car belongs to Jason's father and the other is his mother's. They are featureless four-door sedans, could be last year's or five years old, could be Honda, Toyota—really, who can tell, and who cares? She is not interested in cars. She plans to live in a major city and use public transportation.

But where *did* Jason go, while she stayed patiently on his little boat and the police closed in? Was he hiding in the woods, crouching behind a tree? Did he walk up to the road? Did he have another car in which he drove away? Whose car?

And all those text messages. Did he text somebody to pick him up? Does he realize what's happening to her right now? Does he care?

The policewoman asks again about the gun and the target practice.

She pictures the odd stranded little peninsula. How hot and sticky. How wet and swampy. By now, she thinks, the police must have removed the body.

She flings herself backward from the table. Her free hand flails, shoving away a new and terrible thought. The policewoman is on her feet, prepared for anything.

She does not look at the policewoman. She has a sick view into her own selfish soul.

How can a good, kind person like herself, who intends to help the world, and be a surgeon, and join Doctors Without Borders and save innocent bystanders in civil wars in third-world countries—*how can she be so self-centered that she did not even ask who died in those woods?*

She is crying again. Where do all these tears come from? "Who is it?" she whispers.

"Who is who?"

"The person," she begins. The words fill her with fear. "The person you say—"

That I killed.

But they are only saying this.

It isn't true.

It cannot be true.

To take another human's life is the most dreadful act a person can commit.

She is not that person.

"The person you say was killed," she manages. "Who is it?"

"Derry Romaine."

FRIDAY AFTERNOON

The day is summer slow. Swimming, eating, texting, napping.

Henry, Hayden and Geoffrey show up at the same time. Miranda slides into the river with them and they play water volleyball with an invisible net. Geoffrey has excellent aim and can always send the ball straight to Henry or Hayden. Geoffrey is at ease in the water, as if he'd be a better otter than teenager.

When Geoffrey gets out, he is wrinkly and pruny. He ties an old towel around his waist and climbs the stairs. He does not have the fine muscular shape of Jason Firenza or Derry Romaine. He is just big.

"Bye, Geoffrey!" the little boys chorus.

"Bye, Geoffrey," calls Miranda. "Thanks for playing."

Perhaps this bit of neighborly courtesy will make up for her rudeness on the riding mower.

"Any time," he calls, not turning around.

Miranda and her parents eat supper on the porch. The sun sets very slowly, as if it is enjoying itself. The dusk is soft and friendly. Bats come out. They swoop so fast she can hardly follow the movement. She's glad the bats eat so many bugs and gladder that she is not outside on the grass with them.

Around nine o'clock she takes a long shower, shampooing and conditioning. One delightful thing about a shabby old cottage is that it has shabby old plumbing and therefore big fat pipes with no water-saving devices: the pressure of the heavy flow is practically a massage.

She towels dry, but in the humidity, remains damp.

They do not have air conditioning here.

In their regular house in West Hartford, they set the temperature at 74 for the entire hot-weather season and would never dream of trying to sleep at night except in air conditioning. But at the cottage, they pretend there is a steady breeze off the river that will cool them. *We just need ceiling fans to keep comfortable*, they claim.

Often, this works.

More often, they swelter.

Her father always says he will put in air conditioning when he can afford it, and his daughters always laugh. He can afford anything. He just likes the cottage this way.

Miranda picks out shortie pajamas. She doesn't blow her hair dry. It will air-dry during the night. Now. Decisions. Should she watch baseball with her father in the living room? Curl up on the king-sized bed with her mother, who watches exclusively house and garden shows? Sit on the porch, watching her own favorites on her iPad?

She is shocked to find herself suddenly close to sobbing. Will this be her life? Sharing screens with her mother and father? She wants friends. Well, she has friends, lots of friends, but they're busy and they're in West Hartford.

The awful stab of loneliness won't diminish.

She is standing in the tiny unlit hall between her room and Lander's.

Both are corner rooms. Miranda's two windows open onto the screened porch on one side and the Nevilles' house on the other. Lander's two windows face the Nevilles and the front yard. Through the open window Miranda hears Barrel snuffling and pacing in his run.

She thinks of Lander's crush on Jason Firenza. Does Lander suffer from stabs of loneliness? Are the crowds in which she travels also lonely? Does everyone feel this way now and then?

She stares through Lander's room and out Lander's open front window. Towering trees in full leaf make the front yard utterly dark. Out her own window, the river glitters in the starlight.

A car inches down their driveway.

It must be Jason Firenza bringing Lander home and if

so, it's the first time he's actually approached the house. Miranda tiptoes into her sister's room to watch at an angle, so that she can't be seen. Why am I gathering information about Jason Firenza? she wonders. If ever there was a woman who could take care of herself, it was Lander. Knowing what make of car the guy drives is not going to prove whether or not he's homicidal.

The vehicle is a police car.

Is Jason a cop? No. He would have said so when the trooper was questioning him last Saturday. So is a cop bringing Lander home? Is she drunk? This would be utterly unlike Lander. And realistically, if Lander needs a ride under such circumstances, she would call home.

What are the circumstances?

Lander does not get out of the police car. Neither does Jason.

Two policemen get out.

They are husky, solid men. They are in uniform. They adjust their heavy belts and tug their ties.

Why would the police be here at this hour?

Or any hour?

Icy knowledge comes to Miranda.

There has been a car accident.

If Lander were just hurt, they would call. Actually, the hospital emergency personnel would probably call. There's only one reason for the police to come to the house.

Lander is dead.

Miranda's knees buckle. Her mouth is dry. Her mind swirls.

Out the window she sees a second police car come very slowly down the lane. There is no outdoor lighting, and they cannot see where the driveway leads or where it ends, and they do not want to drive off the cliff.

Has Lander driven off a cliff?

Miranda sits hard on the end of Lander's bed, which will irritate Lander, who makes her bed carefully and tightly every morning.

Oh, Lander! How are we going to be best friends after all? What about your life?

What about medical school and all your work to get there and all your plans?

How will our parents survive this?

She must dress, go into the living room and be a help.

But she is thinking: Did Jason Firenza do this? Is he careless behind a car wheel too? Did he walk away from a car wreck wringing his hands about his passenger's fate, just as he drove a boat away from Derry Romaine?

To capture the breeze, the front door is open. Her parents also see the two police cars come down the drive.

The only one not home is Lander, so the police have to be here about Lander. Her mother flings open the screened door. "Lander!" she cries. "My daughter! Is this about Lander? Is she all right? Was there a car accident? Why are you here?"

The police suggest that they should all sit down.

"Tell me, just tell me!" Her mother's voice is as warbly as an old soprano's and Miranda realizes that this will destroy her mother.

She, Miranda, will not be much consolation. They have staked everything on their older daughter. Miranda does not grieve for herself. It is what it is, and she recognizes it. She grieves for them.

"Nobody is hurt," says one of the policemen.

Miranda is weak with relief. Lander is not dead. She is not even hurt.

But if nobody is hurt, why are there two police cars? Four police officers?

"I think you should sit," says the policeman again.

There are shuffling sounds. Miranda assumes that her parents are on the sofa next to each other, upset and yet relieved.

The officer's voice is a very deep, very loud baritone. It's almost comical. "Is Lander Allerdon your daughter?"

"Yes, yes, of course. Please just tell us what's happening."

"Your daughter is in jail. We received a tip about a delivery of cocaine. We found Lander Allerdon alone on a boat that did in fact have a package of cocaine hidden aboard. In the woods not far from where this boat was tied up, we found the body of a man shot to death. A gun that is probably the murder weapon was found in Lander Allerdon's tote bag. She admits shooting this gun."

5

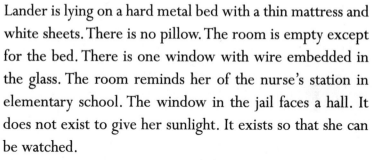

Lander is lying on a hard metal bed with a thin mattress and white sheets. There is no pillow. The room is empty except for the bed. There is one window with wire embedded in the glass. The room reminds her of the nurse's station in elementary school. The window in the jail faces a hall. It does not exist to give her sunlight. It exists so that she can be watched.

A policewoman is standing next to the bed. "You fainted," she says.

Lander tries to think which, of all the ghastly things that are happening, might have caused her to pass out.

"Derry Romaine," says the policewoman. "The man shot in the back in the woods where you were using a gun."

The dead person cannot be Derry Romaine. Derry is

in the hospital. Jason visits him daily. Derry isn't even talking yet. How can Derry be the body in the woods? They're making this up to torture her.

She tries to sit up and nothing happens.

"You're restrained," says the policewoman.

Lander looks sideways. Wide leather bracelets are attached to her wrists, fastening her to the sides of the bed. "This has to be illegal! You can't do this to people!"

"You have a history, Lander. You kicked and hit the officers who brought you in. You tried to bite them."

"I promise not to do that," she whispers.

"Good. But for now, we'll just talk this way."

She closes her eyes instead. "Why am I in a different room?"

"It's not a room. It's a cell."

She cannot bear this vocabulary. "I don't see how it could be Derry Romaine who was killed. He's in the hospital."

"Not now he isn't. He's in the morgue."

How can these people be so cold? How can they talk like this?

"Tell me about the gun, Lander," says the policewoman.

In the little woods, Lander is shocked to see that Jason has a gun; more shocked when he says he loves hunting and shooting. Lander does not know anybody who would make that statement. People in other states say that. States in the South or the West. But here, where it's civilized, where everyone she knows is civilized, no one would think of guns as a hobby. No one would shoot innocent deer or wild turkeys or beautiful pheasants.

Jason laughs. "Connecticut has as many gun enthusiasts as any other state," he says, "not to mention gun manufacturers. And plenty of hunters. You just haven't met any until now. You are one lucky girl. You've met me."

His dancing eyes tease and her heart literally weakens. What matters is whatever Jason wants.

"Come on," he says. "I'll teach you. We'll shoot targets, not squirrels. Don't worry. You won't shed any blood."

But did I shed blood?

"Tell me about the gun," says the policewoman again.

I was laughing, thinks Lander. I was laughing out loud when I aimed.

I killed Derry Romaine.

While I laughed.

FRIDAY NIGHT

The stunned silence in the Allerdon living room is broken by her parents' cries: It isn't true. It's ridiculous. Our daughter has nothing to do with violence or crime. The police have made serious errors. How dare the police do this to our innocent child?

The police repeat their statement.

"Tell us where she is," says Miranda's father. "We have to be with her."

"You can't see her tonight," says the female officer. "She's being processed."

Processed, thinks Miranda. Like sandwich filler. Fingerprints. Searches of body cavities. Mug shots. Interrogations. Handcuffs.

Lander?

Her father's voice is hot with anger. "Our daughter was simply on a date. Jason Firenza took her out. I'm sure he can explain everything."

"She gave us that name. But Jason Firenza was not there when we arrived on the scene. She claims not to know his phone number or address. Can you supply those?"

So it isn't Jason who has been killed, and this is good, because Miranda can imagine a circumstance in which Lander would have to protect herself from Jason Firenza. Once Lander finds out he's a drug dealer, say. But in fact, wouldn't Lander just stomp on him? Yell at him? Call the cops on him?

Miranda cannot visualize her sister in the same room with a gun, let alone using it.

Is Lander protecting Jason? Has Jason killed a man and fled the scene, and Lander is now sacrificing herself for him?

Do people do such things in real life? Would *Lander* do it?

And if Jason isn't dead, who *has* been killed? Whose body have they found?

Why does it take four cops to tell the family that Lander is in this trouble?

Do police routinely run around Connecticut thoughtfully contacting family members when an adult is arrested? Does it take four officers?

Miranda is filled with understanding. It is a hot soupy sensation, as if she has poured hot liquid straight from the stove down her throat.

The police are not here to chat with her parents.

They are here to search the premises of a woman accused of homicide.

In the split second it takes to fathom what the police are saying—that Lander is in jail, accused of drug dealing and murder—Miranda realizes that if there is incriminating material, it is not on a piece of paper. It is on Lander's iPad.

They won't find drugs in Lander's room. Lander has utter scorn for people who use mind-altering substances. People should be proud of their minds and use them for finer purposes than getting stoned. Lander believes that drug cartels in South America and dealers skulking around middle schools are evil. If there are drugs on Jason's boat, Jason put them there without Lander's knowledge.

There's little in Lander's room to search, because the cottage is small, and the family leaves most stuff in West Hartford, hauling in huge L.L.Bean canvas totes or plastic laundry bins what is needed for each stay at the cottage.

The gun theory is ridiculous. Lander has no gun. Would never have a gun. Would never touch a gun if it were around.

But it is possible that Lander knows something. Did she find out about the drug dealing? Discover the fake boat nameplate? Did Jason have some sort of meeting while Lander was there? A delivery? A sale?

Since Lander is never without her cell phone, the police have it now. Any message Lander sent or received is saved on that phone.

But Lander's iPad is here.

Her research, college papers and downloads are on the iPad. Lander is a fine pianist, and tends not to have sheet music but digital copies on her iPad. Her senior-year chemistry project and all its background material are on that iPad. A research project begun in eighth grade involving Lyme disease, because they live at the epicenter of this cruel illness—five years of data and statistics are on that iPad.

And what else?

Something the police should not see?

Miranda also has her iPad at the cottage and she too never travels without it. She uses hers to binge on TV series she has missed. There is nothing of interest to strangers—or for that matter, friends—on Miranda's iPad.

Lander's has a frosted mint-green case that matches her cell phone case. Miranda's case is orange and all fingerprint-y because she's not as careful as her sister and has gotten ink and chocolate on it.

Miranda steps barefoot and silent into Lander's room. She takes the mint-green case off her sister's iPad, carries Lander's tablet into her own room and switches them. Back in Lander's room, she eases the wrong iPad against the tiny magnetic clips of the mint-green case. She leaves it where Lander always does, on the bedside table.

In her own room, she sets Lander's iPad, now in a stained orange cover, on her bed, along with her ereader, a paperback, a cotton sweater, a ponytail holder, a teddy she could not resist from Build-A-Bear, a plate that had cookies and now has crumbs and a cord bracelet she is weaving. Miranda sleeps on the very edge of her bed, one arm hanging down, so that she does not have to move all these precious possessions just because she needs a little sleep.

The police will have a search warrant. It's probably for the entire cottage, not just Lander's room. They will come into Miranda's bedroom too. Better not to be in here watching or her face may give something away. She slips on a summer robe. It is crispy cotton, white with tiny polka dots in primary colors, like the tips of crayons. She loves this robe.

I have to behave normally, she thinks. What is normal when the police in your living room have arrested your sister for murder? When you have just switched case colors so that your parents won't accidentally give away that the police have the wrong iPad?

Barefoot, in her robe, she pads into the living room.

The four police officers fill the room, as if they are the only reason it exists. Around their waists is so much equipment it must bruise their hips. They too are crispy, as if they iron and starch their summer shirts. Two of the men are very bulky. They must spend a lot of time at all-you-can-eat chains. The one woman and the other man are slim. All four stand with their feet slightly apart and their arms slightly away from their bodies, as if to draw weapons. All four, extra pounds or not, look fit.

Her parents are also standing, and they are next to each other behind the sofa, perhaps believing that upholstery will protect them from the news the police have brought.

All eyes look upon Miranda.

"I don't think I heard right," says Miranda, focusing on the nearest officer.

"Focus" is the wrong word. The room blurs with her fear for Lander; fear that she will be caught trying to hide Lander's digital world. The officer is a foot taller than she is, but this is not unusual. Miranda is used to looking up. "You said that my sister—um—my sister . . . ?"

The police gently repeat their statement.

Miranda says sharply, "Lander would never hurt anybody. Ever. And besides, she's very anti-gun. She would never even hold one."

"She admits holding it and shooting it," says the officer. "But she claims she and Jason Firenza were doing target practice and nobody else was there."

Target practice? thinks Miranda. Lander?

"It's a strange location for target practice," says the officer. "It's a strange location, period. And there is a dead body right where Lander admits shooting."

Miranda does not believe this. But the police do. And they have been there. *It's a hunting accident,* she tells herself. "Who was killed?" Her voice splits down the middle, cracking like an old clarinet reed. "Who is the dead person?"

"We haven't identified him yet."

There's no such thing as a person without identification. Everybody has a cell phone and every adult has a wallet.

Did somebody remove the dead man's cell phone and wallet? If so, this cannot be written off as a hunting accident, even if it were deer or turkey season, which it isn't. If the identification is gone, then that murderer walked up to the person he killed, bent down and emptied the pockets. A vision of Lander being there, seeing this, knowing this, is so appalling that Miranda wants to scream and flee all the way to West Hartford. "Lander didn't do that. She just didn't. Jason Firenza must have. Here." She takes her cell phone out of her robe pocket and clicks to the close-up of Jason on their dock, their striped beach towel around his shoulders, their coffee mug in his hand.

A minute ago, Miranda would have said this was just a nicely focused shot of a handsome young man. But even as the officer takes the phone out of her hand to see better, she is frightened. How intimate the photograph looks. How relaxed Jason seems. He could be part of the family.

The officer knows that a fifteen-year-old girl does not take one photo. She takes a series. He asks for permission to scroll through the other photos.

Behave normally, she reminds herself. "Okay."

He studies the photographs. He pauses on the shot where Jason and Lander gaze into each other's eyes. He tilts it for Miranda to see. "They've known each other for a long time, then."

"No, no. That was the first moment they met. That we all met."

"They look very close," says the officer.

This is the same idea Miranda had when she took the shot. "Well, they didn't know each other yet," she says. "Not in that picture. Lander thought he was—um—in shock—and needed—um—a warm wrap. A towel."

But last Saturday was a very hot summer day. Nobody needed a wrap. What the photograph implies is that Lander thought Jason needed affection.

Miranda tells the officer everything. The tug, the barge, the lime-green tow rope, the moment in which Jason cut back on the throttle. She shows him the little video, in which Jason is too far upriver to be recognized, but the tow rope is visible. A green thread against dark water.

The officer scrolls back to the photo of Lander and Jason on the dock looking softly into each other's eyes. "This picture was taken while the water search for Derry Romaine was still happening?" says the officer slowly.

It *is* horrifying that those two beautiful people are exchanging an intimate look while the friend of one of them is drowning. It *is* horrifying that Jason is not out there participating in the search. Miranda is beginning to see why lawyers want the accused to say nothing. The accused's sister is making it worse.

"Miranda, did you tell your sister your belief that Jason Firenza attempted to kill his friend?" asks the officer.

"Yes, of course."

"And what did she say?"

Miranda's answer will matter. All answers matter now. One of the officers is writing everything down. Perhaps what Miranda says will be used against Lander.

Miranda imagines Lander having her rights read to her.

You have the right to remain silent. Anything you say can and will be used against you.

She cannot imagine the terror Lander must be feeling. Nothing is used against people like *us,* thinks Miranda. For people like us, everything is on our side.

Miranda wants her father or her mother to interrupt, but they are as silent as stuffed toys. It feels as if only Miranda and the four police officers are in the room. She needs time to think about Lander's actual answer and whether those words will play well or whether she should make something up or maybe just pretend she has forgotten.

"And what did Lander say when you told her your suspicions?" the cop asks again.

Miranda decides on a careful version of the truth. "Well, Lander isn't usually that impressed with my take on things. And she wasn't impressed by that, either. She told me it was an ugly thought and not to repeat it." This sounds virtuous. Even noble. Miranda is rather pleased.

But the detective says slowly, "She told you not to repeat the possibility that Jason intentionally dumped his friend in the path of a barge?"

And now Miranda's quote is laden with implications. Lander doesn't want anybody else to think this. Why not? Because it's true? Because Lander knows it's true?

"Why did Jason motor right up to *your* dock on the day of the barge incident?"

Because Lander waved a big striped beach towel at him,

thinks Miranda. But she does not say this. It sounds like a signal, as if the whole thing really was prearranged.

She knows what the next question will have to be. *Why did Jason arrive at any dock at all when he should have been out there searching for his drowning companion?*

Time to stop talking. Miranda turns to her parents. "Lander needs a lawyer, I think."

The police do not remark on this, but produce their search warrant. Her father takes it, unbelieving. It is in an envelope and he cannot get it out. His fingers are stiff with shock. He has trouble reading the words. He is incapacitated by what is happening.

Miranda shows them Lander's room. When they turn on the ceiling light, they see a small very tidy space, with a single bed neatly made, a small white chest of drawers, a small white bedside table and a mint-green iPad. There are paperbacks on a wall shelf, a wire tote filled with cosmetics and shampoo hanging on the back of the door, a large canvas bag sagging empty in the corner and decorative cardboard boxes lined up on the single shelf in the tiny closet, in which the police will find a small selection of designer sunglasses, caps, hair accessories, scarves and CDs.

"This is all she owns?" the detective asks incredulously.

"This is our summer place. Most of our stuff is in West Hartford."

He texts, probably asking for another search warrant for West Hartford.

They start in one corner of the room. They move, lifting and opening everything. Perhaps they are looking for drugs.

It's the one thing she knows they will not find. She goes back into the living room. Her dazed parents hold out their arms and the three Allerdons stand together, loosely linked. She feels like the illustration of an atom—her thoughts like electrons racing around in their orbits, getting nowhere.

The minute the police pick up the iPad they find in Lander's room, they will flick to email. Miranda herself rarely uses email. It's work to write an email. But she gets quite a few because teachers send assignments, the choral director sends rehearsal reminders, the church youth director sends field trip instructions.

All these will be addressed to Miranda.

The police will then flip open the iPad in Miranda's room and see that *it's* the one they want.

If she's lucky, though, they won't start their iPad research while they're in the house or in the driveway. It's now ten o'clock in the evening. They must be tired. They must want to go to bed. If she's lucky, they will drive to some headquarters and deposit the iPad there, planning to work on it in the morning. Miranda will have the night to do her own—

Her own what?

What is she doing? Why is she doing it? Now there will be two sisters in trouble. And it will totally look as if Miranda is covering for Lander. As if Miranda has reason to believe Lander has done bad things.

Her desperate parents sit on the sofa and open their contact lists. They try to think of somebody to phone. They have no knowledge of criminal lawyers. And how can they possibly say to a close friend, neighbor or business acquaintance, *Our daughter has been arrested for murder and we need help?*

Murder. The most terrible thing a person can do.

A life is cruelly ended. A human being shot or stabbed or run over. Murder is irrevocable. There is no do-over.

Oh, Lander, thinks Miranda.

The police search the bathroom, but it's so little and stripped down that this takes hardly a minute. They glance into Miranda's room, the kitchen, her parents' room. They do not search. The only thing they take away is the wrong iPad.

As the police walk to the front door, Miranda's mother gets up, panting and brushing away hot tears. "We have to see Lander. Tell us exactly where she is. We're driving down there."

The burly officer with the very deep voice shakes his head. "There's a lot to do in a homicide. I'm not sure when you can see her. Call tomorrow morning. But tomorrow afternoon is more likely. Maybe you can coax your daughter to talk to us. She isn't saying anything."

"But isn't silence best?" asks Miranda's father, eyes darting around, as if he hopes to find an escape route from this nightmare.

"It might be," agrees the officer, implying that since Lander is guilty, the less she says, the safer she is.

Lander. A killer.

Horror crowds up against them, sneering.

Miranda wants the last word. "Look for Jason Firenza," she orders them. "He did it."

"We haven't found him," admits the officer. "In fact, there doesn't seem to be anybody by that name in Connecticut."

I didn't find him either, Miranda remembers. But he's out there. I will not let him disappear. He's guilty. I'm finding him.

The last officer out the door pauses. He says gently, "Reporters and TV stations like to cover homicides. Brace yourselves. This will be on the morning news, online and in the morning paper."

The police are gone.

Her parents shudder, deny that this is happening and beg God to make it end.

Miranda sits cross-legged on the sofa, staring at the crowded screen of Lander's iPad.

Icon after icon. Folders and files by the dozen. It would take weeks to make a dent in this. She scans the last few days of emails, but Lander does not email much and there is nothing personal.

Lander has not tweeted lately. Why not? Is she so busy with Jason she doesn't have a minute? But that's not possible. Their lives are geared around communication. Texting, tweeting, Snapchat—they come first, not last. Is Jason so exciting she doesn't care about anybody else?

Or has Lander learned a dark secret? The first fact of her existence that she cannot share?

Lander's Facebook page, however, has loads of pictures. It looks as if Lander spends most of her time with Jason, photographing him. The photos are visible only to Lander's friends. The police, should they go to her Facebook page—presumably they already have, on their own computers—cannot see this.

The authorities can probably circumvent this easily. But how interested will the police be in tracking Jason down? Not very, since they think they have the killer in custody.

Once Lander's arrest is on television and in the papers, and people are tweeting the news and sharing it, everybody out there will Google Lander Allerdon. All of eastern Connecticut will click over and take a look at Lander's Facebook page.

If Derry Romaine goes to college in Connecticut—and that's still iffy—perhaps Jason does, too. For sure, Jason lives around here and keeps boats here. Somebody somewhere in Connecticut knows Jason. Somebody somewhere in Connecticut knows where to find him.

It's a matter of letting that person know that Miranda needs the information.

Miranda will post her own photograph of Jason Firenza on Lander's Facebook page. She will include a caption. *This man calls himself Jason Firenza, but that is not his name.*

He murdered somebody. Lander has wrongly been arrested for that murder. Please help Lander. Please identify him.

Lander has privacy controls. Only her 347 friends can see the content. To advertise Jason Firenza, Miranda needs to open that site to the world. And that means she has to change the privacy controls.

She may or may not know Lander's password. When Lander got her first iPad, Miranda was not old enough to be given one, and she was miserable with envy and grief. Amazingly, her big sister let Miranda cuddle up for a few minutes as Lander experimented with her new prize. Miranda watched Lander enter pass codes. At the time, Lander used her own name and the numbers of her birthday, August 6. L8AND6ER.

Years have passed.

Is Lander the type to change her password on a regular basis?

Yes.

In fact, Lander is the type to purchase a password app, so that the app itself assigns new alphanumeric codes every so often.

Lander, for once in your life, don't be anal. Cherish your first password so much that you never change it!

She carefully enters L8AND6ER.

Yes!

Miranda almost shouts with joy. Instead she grits her teeth so that her parents will be aware of nothing. Actually, her parents *aren't* aware of anything. They are frozen, blinded, by what has socked them.

A minute of editing and Lander no longer has privacy. Everybody in the world who looks her up on Facebook can see everything.

Lander will hate this. She will hate Miranda for doing it.

Her parents are mumbling the same things over and over. *This can't be true. This is a bad dream.*

Maybe it is. Maybe Miranda will wake up Saturday morning, having taken irrevocable steps of her own, naming Jason Firenza as a murderer. Maybe even now, the police have seen their error and are letting Lander go.

Miranda cannot publicize this nightmare before the world publicizes it. During the night, it might all solve itself. And if Miranda posts this—why, the medical school might read it! Reject Lander. Miranda will have ruined Lander's future.

She needs a second opinion.

Her parents are hopeless. They can't even make themselves call a close neighbor in West Hartford who is a judge and surely knows criminal lawyers.

"It's after midnight," says Miranda's mother. "We never phone people at this hour."

"Mom, it's a murder," says Miranda. "Don't worry about waking anybody up. Make the call."

But although Miranda can be firm about what her parents should do, she cannot be firm about what *she* ought to do. She wants to call Candy and talk, but she does not want to say out loud the horrible claims of the police. She thinks of texting, but it's too huge for a few thumb taps.

The night passes.

Lander has two national papers on her tablet. Miranda adds two local papers and two local TV stations, Hartford and New Haven, and watches them endlessly. Waiting for the worst.

Around two in the morning, Miranda goes to bed. She doesn't turn on a light. The screen of Lander's iPad is enough to see by.

She lies there endlessly checking the local news. There is no risk of falling asleep. She is pumped with fear for Lander and rage at Jason Firenza.

At four a.m., the website of the Hartford television station displays a new banner. WEST HARTFORD WOMAN ARRESTED IN RIVERSIDE MURDER.

It's not a bad dream. It's real.

There are two photographs.

One is from the high school yearbook. Lander looks like a million other pretty blond high school girls. Her character and brilliance do not show. When people gaze at this, they will think, *So even in rich suburbia, girls go wrong. What kind of parents raise a monster who deals in cocaine and kills for it?*

The second photograph is a mug shot. Lander has been crying. Her hair is tangled. Her eyes are open so wide that Miranda actually wonders if her anti-drug sister is on something.

Miranda goes to Facebook.

Her hands are quivering.

Miranda's accusation that Jason Firenza is a murderer appears on Facebook at 4:10 a.m. on Saturday morning.

6

Night passes. Down the corridors of the jail, the lights are dimmed, but in Lander's cell, the light does not go out. She sleeps a few minutes now and then, but mostly she lies there, knotted with fear and grief.

The sheet is rough. At home, she sleeps on five-hundred-count percale. She may never sleep on that again. She may never even see it again. She may never go to a department store and buy new sheets, or try on shoes, or stop at the makeup counters and get her face done.

She cannot tell the time. She does not wear a watch. They have taken her cell phone.

She misses her cell phone more than any one person. How sick is that?

She thinks a lot about Miranda. Her sister warned her

several times. *He's dangerous, Lanny, don't go anywhere with him.* But it is Lander's habit to ignore Miranda.

She ignores *every* warning. A good physician constantly considers warning signs in patients; medicine is probably all about warning signs. But she, Lander, scorns them.

She is a Valentine's Day cartoon, shot by a snickering cupid. It is love that has brought her down. Even now, in this hideous lonely night, her fear, horror and shame are less important than her love for Jason. There has to be an explanation. One where she can still love him, and he will still love her.

But the police are correct to be skeptical. Who doesn't know her boyfriend's cell phone number? Who doesn't know his email address? Who doesn't follow him on Twitter?

How can she possibly be unable to name the make of the cars in which he drives her? Why does she not question Jason when they take more than one boat from more than one marina?

And as for their final trip, weaving down tiny brooks that carve the acres of marsh along the eastern edge of the river, why does she not question every bit of this? They pointlessly circle from Lander's house to the marina, down the highway, across the I-95 Connecticut River bridge and back up the other side. Then they stop at a flood-ugly swamp, with rotting driftwood and muddy banks, perhaps the only place on the river that is not beautiful. And then he talks her into target shooting? Really?

But he doesn't have to talk her into anything. She is so in love she would kill for him.

She hears this thought and wants to scrape her fingernails through her brain.

I didn't think that, she tells herself. *I did not kill for him. Or did I?*

She wants to scream. In another cell, a woman does scream, hour after hour, and also bangs her head against a wall. The police keep shouting at her to stop. Eventually they fasten her to some sort of chair, telling her it's for her own good, and the woman screams, "It takes four of you, doesn't it? I hate you! Get me out of this chair! I'll never stop screaming!" But she does stop. Because of exhaustion, a gag or an injection?

Lander wants to stop practically everything. She wants to stop her own thoughts. Stop being here. Stop loving Jason. Stop being without her cell phone.

Does she truly love Jason? Or does she love being asked?

Her heart is ill with how much she wants Jason to show up and get her out of this. She imagines all sorts of dramatic scenes, from his confession to storming the jail.

But if she really did shoot the gun that really did kill Derry Romaine, nothing can save her. And maybe nothing should. Murderers should not get off.

She prays over and over. God, please, please, please, get me out of here. This is not my life.

She knows it's morning only because trays are delivered

to a cell out of sight. A furious male voice shouts, "Call that breakfast? Call that coffee?" This is followed by a stream of obscenities.

She hasn't been here twenty-four hours and already jail is so hard she cannot bear it.

Lander is used to control over her own time. Time is her arena, to do with as she chooses. But time and meals now belong to her jailers.

If they find her guilty of murder, she will have nothing but time. Armloads, years, decades of time. Hard time, it's called, and she can see already why that adjective is used.

She does not move when a tray of food and liquid is placed in her cell. It is all she can do not to throw up at the smell of it. She clenches muscles from her jaw to her belly, to keep from screaming. Because things can get worse. They can strap you to a torture chair. Down the hall, the angry man hurls his hot coffee at his jailer and Lander totally identifies with that decision.

The policewoman comes for her again.

Lander doesn't blink, as if being motionless will protect her; as if she is prey and the predators will not spot her if she is frozen in place.

"Lander," says the policewoman sharply. "Get up. Come."

These are commands given to dogs. Lander is no longer a bright, beautiful vision of a brilliant future physician. She is a dog in a crate.

"Lander!" yells the policewoman.

From the unseen cells come cheers. "Hey, Lander!"

screams a female voice. "Fight back! You show 'em, girl! You a killer! You don't do what some cop ask!"

Lander is paralyzed.

These strangers know what she's accused of? How can they know? Who else knows? Does the world know? Do her parents know?

The voice from the cell is not jeering. The voice is entertained. Lander is a sideshow.

My arrest is online, thinks Lander. On TV news. People are tweeting.

"My" arrest. As if she possesses it. But she doesn't. The arrest belongs to the police. Her whole life belongs to the police now.

She approaches the bars of her cell. It's not a long walk. This is a tiny compartment. She dimly recognizes the police-woman from yesterday.

"Turn around."

Lander turns around.

The door is opened. Handcuffs encircle her wrists again. The heavy cuffs are not on her wrists solely to control her. They are reminders. *You are in jail.*

Without hands, she is as helpless as a swaddled infant.

In the corridor, the air conditioning is arctic. She tries to lift her chin and be brave, but she is dirty and needs a shower. Her hair is a mess, her clothes are wrinkled and she has no hands. The construction of the hall is also cement block and the word "block" springs up in her face, shouting, *Prison block, prison block.*

Can my life dissolve like this? Just slide down the drain?

She is aware of her selfishness, thinking only of how hard this is on her. Grotesquely, she is thinking more about the loss of her cell phone than the death of Derry Romaine.

They pass the women's holding cell. A half dozen females—skinny, fat, white, black, wearing tiny little skirts or big sagging sweat suits—are sprawled alone in misery or standing alone in rage.

A woman missing a front tooth presses her face against the bars and grins at Lander. She has the wildest eyes and the most chaotic hair Lander has ever seen. "You liked the blood, Lander? You liked doing it?" the woman screeches.

Lander is terrified.

When the corridor takes a sharp right turn and the holding cell is out of sight, Lander says to the policewoman, "Thank you for protecting me from those women. Thank you for keeping me in a different"—she can't say the word "cell"—"place."

"Those women are charged with shoplifting and prostitution, Lander," says the cop. "*You're* charged with murder. You're in a separate cell to protect *them*."

SATURDAY MORNING

At six a.m., on the theory that a jail is always open, and so it will not be rude to call early, Miranda's parents phone. When may they see their daughter?

They are told to call again in the afternoon.

The day stretches hideously ahead. They decide to drive back to West Hartford. They have to find a lawyer.

Her parents assume that Miranda will come too. They should be a unit. Three is stronger than two. But she has a sense of needing to hold down the fort; a sense that the cottage is going to be their strength and somebody must stay.

"I'll be fine here," says Miranda.

Her parents stare at her. They are not able to think anything through. Her mother looks gaunt and yellow. Her father looks thick and gray.

She hugs them. "You concentrate on what you have to do."

Her dazed parents nod. By six-thirty, they are driving away and Miranda is alone. It's no different from many days at the cottage, when her father commutes to work and her mother heads out for errands or volunteer hours. Miranda's fifteen, after all.

But a sister in jail changes everything. A murder down-river changes everything.

The cottage does not feel like a fort. It feels empty. She feels as if she has always lived alone here; will always be alone here.

Miranda doesn't usually get out of her pajamas for hours on a Saturday morning, but now the shortie pajamas make her feel vulnerable. She slips into tight jeans and a loose shirt. The taut denim and long sleeves feel better.

She goes out on the porch and her beloved river looks evil. Dark and gray and hiding things. A color Lander generally refers to as "oil spill." Miranda goes back in and curls up on the big sofa, protecting her back with fat pillows.

She holds Lander's iPad in her lap. One look at that mug shot of Lander staring in tearful panic at the camera, and Miranda too is in a state of tearful panic.

But mainly, Miranda's state is exhaustion. She has not slept. The intensity of her fear for Lander and the decision to use Facebook to find a killer have sapped her. She falls asleep. The heat of the new day crawls through the open windows and the screened doors. The ceiling fan slowly turns above her face.

The clouds disappear and the sun boils.

The sound of a closing door penetrates her sleep, but not enough to wake her, since coming and going through the porch is a constant.

There are other sounds. Water running. The door again.

She sleeps, thick and deep, and then snaps awake, sleep broken like ice with a hammer.

She's the only one home. Who is closing doors and running water?

She leaps up. Darts from room to room. She is alone.

She races to the porch and sees no one.

She goes outside, letting the screened door bang, and stands at the top of the cliff stairs.

Nobody is there.

But the big dark carry bag for Stu's inflatable kayak is on the dock, and a towel she recognizes as Geoffrey's.

One of them came in to use the bathroom or get water from the kitchen sink.

Miranda is used to the comings and goings of neighbors. Now she is shivering, as with fever.

Anybody could plant something in Lander's room.

She stares up and down the river, trying to spot Stu or Geoffrey. Who are they, anyway? Who is anybody, when the sister you think you know gets caught up in a murder and has a missing boyfriend who never existed to start with?

She pours herself a cup of coffee from her father's carafe, adds a lot of sugar and so much milk that she has to reheat it in the microwave. It's just the way Barrel likes his coffee and she is suddenly desperate for company, even doggy company. Maybe especially doggy company.

She considers her plan, which depends on other people telling her where and who Jason really is. She taps the local TV station icon on Lander's screen. In the state of Connecticut, the most interesting thing going on is the arrest of Lander Allerdon for murder. Lander is the first banner, the first article, the first photograph. They have no video so far, but they do have a bright-eyed reporter standing in front of a building, claiming that Lander is behind these bars. The reporter refers to Lander as a "woman from West Hartford," which sounds like some strange adult rather than Miranda's older sister.

They have found a more recent picture of Lander than her posed high school graduation photo. Lander is receiving a certificate of merit in chemistry at her college. She is gorgeous, smiling with pride. The mug shot is even more shocking next to that. How did that beautiful academic star turn into a ruined, scared, drugged-out killer?

Henry and Hayden charge up the porch stairs and fling open the wooden screened door, which bangs against the siding. "Hi, Miranda!" they scream.

The Warren family does not get cable television. On their computers, they watch DVDs suitable for small children. They never look at the news. Mr. and Mrs. Warren feel that it will only upset them and since they can have no effect on it, why bother? They know nothing about America, the world or the economy, let alone Lander. They do not worry about their innocent children being in the house of an accused murderer.

Miranda has a cloudy thought that Lander's situation is all about water. River, boats, docks. The nightmare starts here, on her stretch of river, below these other houses. Could these neighbors be part of it? She could check Facebook pages. Find clues. Maybe there are posts from sellers of drug paraphernalia. Or coded messages to meet in a strange place at a strange time.

As if a drug dealer would announce it for the world to read.

She is glad to have the distraction of hungry little boys. There is no mystery in Henry and Hayden. But they are born spies, up in that tree house. What should she ask? With her mind on the banging porch door and the possessions of Geoffrey and Stu littering the dock, she says casually, "Henry, how well do you know Geoffrey and Stu?"

"What do you mean?" asks Henry. "I know where they live."

"Well, but do they—" Miranda tries to think of a way to interrogate Henry. "Do they visit your house?"

"Our house?" repeats Henry.

Miranda tries to phrase her questions better. "What do you hear from Stu's parents in Australia?"

Henry giggles. "My parents think they are not in Australia. They think Stu buried them in the basement."

Miranda objects. "The houses on that side of the street don't have basements. They're built on bedrock."

Hayden says, "We have a basement."

A verbal contribution from Hayden is rare. "What do you keep down there?" asks Miranda.

"The furnace," says Hayden.

Miranda means to ask about Geoffrey next but already she is out of interrogation energy. How do the police do it—endlessly ask questions from people who don't have intelligent answers? Of course it would help if Miranda had intelligent questions.

The boys beg for pancakes.

Miranda usually pours out one big circle, adding a tablespoon of batter on each side for ears and anything she can find for eyes: raisins, Craisins, marshmallows. It is difficult to assemble the ingredients. She stands there blinking, trying to remember how this is done.

The egg she retrieves from the refrigerator falls out of her hand and smashes on the floor.

The boys are already watching cartoons. Miranda's TV is sometimes more appealing than Miranda.

Cleaning up the egg is a huge task. She has to squat and once she is down, her heart is down too.

My sister is under arrest for murder, Miranda thinks.

She admits using the murder weapon.

Miranda's mother texts. They have arrived at the West Hartford house. The police have also arrived, with another search warrant. The police will have their work cut out for them. It's a very large house for a family with a whole lot of stuff.

Have the police already started on the iPad they wrongly think is Lander's? They will be back at the cottage the minute they open Miranda's iPad. If she is to do anything more than post Jason Firenza's photo on Facebook, she has to do it now.

But a brain too foozled to mop up a broken egg is not ready to think up hashtags for Instagram or Tumblr. Lander loves Twitter but Miranda cannot come up with a plan for using her sister's Twitter account.

The front door is open. It's the first thing they do in the morning—fling open the front door to get cross-ventilation. The air is already sticky. It's going to be another hot day. And Miranda is brain-dead.

Her mother texts again. They have spoken to the attorney who wrote their wills. He is calling around to find a criminal attorney.

Miranda is proud of her parents, finding the courage to make that dreadful call: *Our daughter has been accused of murder.*

Miranda does not have the courage to call Candy. She doesn't even have the guts to read her messages. She is still hoping this isn't real. Talking will make it real. Besides, if she and Candy thrash it all out, detail after detail, Miranda will have a friend but accomplish nothing. She must find Jason Firenza.

She watches the local station on Lander's iPad. They are thrilled to have this exciting story in their backyard. The anchors struggle for the stern, sad expressions required of reporters covering homicides. In fact, they are exultant. One reporter cannot keep the joy out of her voice when she says, "It is known that the only fingerprints on the murder weapon are the fingerprints of the accused, Lander Allerdon."

The only fingerprints! thinks Miranda. *Oh, Lander! What happened?*

Henry and Hayden watch cartoons with an open-mouthed, hypnotized expression that Miranda finds slightly frightening. They are entirely inside the world of the TV show.

They are not company. They are just here.

Jack appears at the front door. The ragged screen has tears in it and the door itself doesn't quite fit anymore. Like everything in the cottage, it needs work. It's not a barrier for insects and not for people. And yet it stops Jack. "Hi, Miranda! Can I come in?"

His parents must be as clueless as Henry and Hayden's or they would never let him come to the house of an accused murderer.

It seems to Miranda she lives on a street filled with clueless parents. Jack never talks about his mother and father, who are divorced and remarried and hostile; Jack is always getting out of somebody's car and telling them not to worry and then slamming the door and chugging into the other parent's house without looking back.

What do these four people do, other than trade Jack? Miranda has no idea. She has no idea what Mr. and Mrs.

Warren do either, although supposedly it's something to do with computers. You would think people who use computers to earn a living would check the news now and then. Read the headlines, anyway.

"Come on in," she hollers to Jack. She is still in the kitchen, as if her feet are stuck to the floor. And perhaps they are. She hasn't mopped up all the egg.

Since checking on the neighbors is the only course of action that occurs to her, even if it is a stupid course of action, she starts with Henry and Hayden's parents on Facebook. Their page features artsy photographs of the boys. But unless they friend her, Miranda can see nothing more.

Nightmare.

Miranda does not want adults around. Once they're there, they're there, invading her space. They might even post.

Jack punches Henry and Hayden, who joyfully punch back but do not take their eyes off the cartoons. Jack comes into the kitchen and says softly, "It was probably self-defense."

Which means Jack knows about Lander and he believes that Lander did shoot the man; he just isn't categorizing it as murder.

Through the long terrible night, Miranda and her parents stared at each other, saying, *No, no, no, no, it can't be true,* but they did not discuss the actual murder. They had no information about the actual murder. But now Miranda has knowledge from the TV reports, and somehow it's easy to talk to Jack. "The man was shot in the back," says Miranda. "How self-defense-y is that?"

Jack nods. "I know, but I can't think of anything else. I mean, Lander is scary enough already. She doesn't need a gun."

Jack is twelve. He is an awkward boy, although not as awkward as Geoffrey, who is fifteen, and nowhere near as awkward as Stu, who is twenty-three. Maybe it's something in the water.

She remembers the running water she heard in her dream, and her waking assumption that it was Geoffrey or Stu. But really, it could have been anybody. Somebody could have tied up at the dock, scrambled up the stairs . . .

This is fried brain talking. In her whole life she has never heard of trespassing by dock.

Jack says, "Have you talked to her yet? Lander? Is she— well, I know she can't be okay, but is she—like—*okay*?"

The comic aspect of friending adult neighbors recedes.

Lander is not okay. She is in jail. She may never get out of jail. A man is dead. He has been murdered. He has been shot in the back.

It is only because Miranda met the police herself—heard their voices—saw their uniforms and weapons—watched their lights whirl on their cop car—that she can believe this is actually happening to her very own family.

Lander is now part of a world that belongs on television: one of those half-reality, half-reenactment crime shows. Bad photography, clumsy filming, blurry faces.

And Miranda is standing around worrying about Facebook friends? She makes the friend request to Mrs. Warren. To Jack, she says, "The murderer is that guy Jason Firenza. The one playing chicken with the barge. Which turns out not to be his name. There's no such person. Even the police can't find a person named Jason Firenza."

"I know. I saw Lander's Facebook page. You put that photo and that request on there?"

"Yes."

"Way to go," compliments Jack. "Let's see if you have responses yet."

What a failure she is as an investigator. It's been hours since posting that accusation and she hasn't looked yet to read the responses! *Oh, Lanny, I want to help, I'm trying to help, I'm sorry I'm so stupid.*

Lander's Facebook page is filled with posts. Friends denying that Lander could ever have done such a thing. Friends offering to help. Strangers commenting on previous posts of Lander's, which apparently include views of her body that she should never have put online. Strangers claiming evidence that Lander is the killer is piling up, and this accusation of somebody else is libel.

No one provides the real identity of Jason Firenza.

But the real identity of the dead man is now known. He is Derry Romaine.

Miranda's horror doubles. I probably *did* see Jason Firenza cut back on the throttle. He probably did hope the barge would kill Derry. But his murder attempt failed. Six days later, Derry was murdered by bullet.

Could Lander have been so hypnotized by Jason that she agreed to fire the bullet? Impossible! But then how did it happen? Why did it happen?

Miranda's cell phone peals with her mother's ring tone. Something too big for a text message.

"Honey, I'm driving down to the shoreline so I can meet the defense lawyer," says her mother. The speech is fast and frantic. "Daddy is staying here. He doesn't want to leave the house while the police are searching it and anyway he's got to raise a lot of money and we're not sure how. The lawyer has to have money up front. I'm absolutely panicked about the money."

Miranda is taken aback that the conversation is about money rather than Lander.

Lander has complained more than once that their parents are far too concerned with money; it's not good for people to think so much about money.

Lander is correct. She is in the world's worst trouble, and all their parents can think about is money.

Miranda rarely considers money.

When the topic of wealth comes up, her father always says that they are "comfortable." Indeed, Miranda's life is so comfortable she can hardly imagine leaving for college; the way she lives now is the exact way she always wants to live.

"You can't just write a check?" asks Miranda.

"We could if we had anything in our checking account." There is a funny choking pause. Her mother is trying not to sob. "We live beyond our means, Rimmie. We always have. It's more fun. We have no savings. We have huge debts. Mortgages, car payments, lots of credit cards. Everything depends on everything working. And now, when something is really wrong, and it's going to be really expensive, we have nothing to fall back on. We can't even get loans on the houses because we already have such big loans." Miranda's mother pauses. And then in her normal calm Mother-knows-all voice, she says, "Don't worry about it, Rimmie. We'll solve it."

"I love you, Mom," whispers Miranda, but she is staring at a terrifying invisible truth. Love does not raise money.

There will be no way to get Lander out of trouble without money.

They have no money.

Miranda is still listening to her mother on her cell phone, but she is also looking at the iPad, because when a screen is active, Miranda finds it difficult to look away.

Either Mrs. Warren really does work at a computer and checks her activity log constantly, or she has nothing to do all day except hope somebody gets in touch, because the friend acceptance has already come through.

Miranda taps the Warren page.

She has never seen a Facebook page so covered with faces: Henry's face, Hayden's face; their faces at birthday parties and nature walks and Disney World; their faces being painted at a fair; their faces asleep.

Mrs. Warren posts only about her sons. How brilliant, handsome and interesting they are. Her female friends post the same about their children. They're all basically saying, *Yeah, your little boy can use a fork, fine—but my little boy multiplies four-digit numbers.*

The site does not seem to be a cover for the sick activity of drug dealing on the Connecticut River.

Miranda looks at the same two little boys sitting fifteen feet away and is overwhelmed. Is this to be her life? Suspecting nice people? Thinking evil of them?

What is her point?

The point is to identify Jason Firenza and get him in trouble, instead of Lander. The Warrens have nothing to do with anything.

Jack is talking on his own cell to his cousin Tanner, a girl apparently on the cutting edge of computer communications. She is instructing him in the use of Vine, on which he will put the little video of the lime-green tow rope. Tanner has decided that the hashtag for everything will be #LanderAllerdon. That's what the world is going to check.

On the phone, Miranda's mother drones on about raising money.

"Lemme use the iPad," whispers Jack. She nods, and he takes it into the living room, saying into his own phone, "Tanner, what will it accomplish to show the video? Rimmie was so far away when she filmed the powerboat that you can't recognize Jason Firenza."

Miranda would like to hear Tanner's answer, but her mother says, "There's no other choice, Rimmie. We'll have to sell one of the houses."

Sell one of the houses?

Miranda knows immediately that no one will buy the West Hartford house. It is a big rambling old place built in the 1930s, in a style called Tudor, which means it has timber framing on the outside, huge chimneys and small windows. It is costly to heat. It has no walk-in closets. It has no granite countertops. It's not on the best street. It doesn't have the best yard. It would take a fortune to fix up.

But the cottage might actually sell overnight. It has a world-class view. It is waterfront. There is a legal dock, however small. It has a beautiful acre and a half of sloping land, with magnificent trees and thickets of native mountain laurel and rhododendron. Weekenders—not just from Hartford, but also Boston and New York—love this location.

Sell the cottage.

Jack is now chatting with Tanner about the best utilization of Lander's Twitter account.

Her mother says, "Shall I swing by the cottage and get you on my way to the shoreline?"

The Connecticut River is a serious barrier. Picking up Miranda will add a lot of time to the journey. And what use will Miranda be? Will the defense lawyer even want the little sister there? Certainly Lander never wants the little sister there.

Miranda forgets how frightened she was a few hours ago. The house is full of little boys, noise and pancake mix. In a minute this girl Tanner will have a plan of action and anyway, Miranda does not want to be in a car with her mother, listening to this awful talk of dollars. "I'm fine, Mom," she says. "Don't make the detour for me."

Through the open front door and the torn screen, Miranda sees a large four-door silver sedan coming down the drive. It is an old Crown Victoria, a model frequently used by the state police.

She grabs Jack's shoulder and whispers, "Take the iPad, go home and do everything Tanner tells you."

Jack frowns, unwilling to cooperate.

Nobody ever wants to leave the Allerdon cottage. It has a pull for the neighborhood that Miranda loves. To be the center of activity is as wonderful as the river itself.

When the cottage is sold, the buyer will tear it down and build a mansion worthy of the site. Part of the reason kids swarm here is that the house is all but a shack. It is built for fun by the river. Its purpose is summer. The other reason is that her parents love kids. They love feeding them and reading to them, playing badminton or catch with them and dragging out the keg of Legos for them.

Gone. It will all be gone.

The Crown Vic parks. The doors open. A tall man wearing a suit and tie gets out of the passenger side. Miranda has not seen him before. She doesn't want to see him now.

"The police are here," she whispers to Jack. She taps the iPad. "This is what they want. I tricked them. I switched my iPad with Lander's. They left yesterday with mine."

The driver of the Crown Vic also gets out. He too is wearing a suit and tie.

Miranda calls to Henry. "Go answer the front door, Henry. Tell them I'll be there in a minute!"

Jack is full of admiration. "Rimmie, you are something!"

Her mother is saying, "But selling a house is very slow. We have to find a whole lot of cash somewhere else and we have to find it fast."

Miranda pushes Jack to the screened porch. "Hurry," she breathes. The overgrown mountain laurel, climbing roses and rhododendron will hide Jack when he slips out the back. She will stand at the front door, keeping the police attention on herself, making sure they don't glimpse Jack and what he has in his hand.

She is turning everything over to Jack and his unknown cousin Tanner. But if anybody gets in trouble, it will be her, not Jack. He's only twelve. What does he know?

Actually, he knows a lot. He is brilliant on a computer. What will he find? Will he find Jason Firenza?

Or proof that Lander does know about the drug dealing?

And if they do find Jason Firenza, what about the fact that only Lander touched the gun and only Lander's fingerprints are on it?

What if finding Jason Firenza makes it worse?

What if Jason Firenza vanished because he saw Lander kill Derry, and he does not want to testify against her?

I do not believe that, Miranda tells herself. *I will not believe that. Jason Firenza tried to murder Derry on the river last Saturday and yesterday he succeeded in murdering Derry with a gun and my sister is an innocent bystander, and I don't care about fingerprints. So there.*

"So we're calling relatives," says Miranda's mother.

Miranda crosses the living room floor. She tries not to burst into tears. If her parents are steeling themselves to call family and beg for cash, she can face down some state trooper.

The front porch is not screened. Big old rockers and sagging wicker chairs wait comfortably in the shade. Henry chats happily with the two men, who remain on the grass just below the steps. Hayden sucks his thumb.

Sell the cottage.

If the cottage is sold, it will kill Miranda.

No, actually. It won't.

A man *has* been killed. That is the point.

Henry is explaining to the police that he lives a few houses upriver and that Miranda babysits for him and his little brother all the time.

Miranda comes to the door.

They introduce themselves. They are detectives.

Not the local constables. Not the resident state trooper.

Detectives.

Their goal is to find evidence that will incriminate Lander. "Are your parents home, Miranda?" they ask courteously.

They haven't met Miranda, but they know who she is.

"No. I'm actually on the phone with my mother right now. Mom?" she says into her cell phone. "I think that sounds like a good plan. And if we have to sell a house, it has to be the cottage. I can call a real estate agent. You want me to do that while you do the lawyer?"

"Oh, my darling girl, you are so wonderful. Let's wait a day or two. I think your father will find enough money for a retainer, so that at least the lawyer can visit the jail and handle the arraignment."

"Arraignment." What a terrifying word. Full of judges and cells with bars.

How can this be happening to Lander?

Miranda swallows in horror. "Give Lander a hug for me." It occurs to her that they might not be *able* to hug Lander; that her parents may have to speak through bars or bulletproof glass.

She slides the phone into her jeans pocket and waves hostess-fashion at the chairs and rockers. "Please sit down," she says to the detectives.

"Miranda, we have the search warrant. We need to get in and look around."

"Maybe when my parents get home."

"The warrant gives us permission."

Miranda pretends she has never watched television, has no idea what a warrant is, wasn't around last night and can't fathom what's going on. But seven-year-old Henry, who supposedly does not watch any rough, violent TV, says firmly, "Rimmie, once they go to a judge and get a warrant, it's all over. They have to come in."

"I don't think so," says Miranda. "I think there are times when they can't, like when a grown-up isn't home."

The detectives ask Henry if *his* parents are home. They don't want little boys around while they detect.

"No, they're never home," explains Henry. "We're always here."

This is a wild exaggeration but it certainly distracts the detectives. Miranda doesn't clear things up. Besides, it's never been clear. Where *are* Mr. and Mrs. Warren all the time?

Geoffrey chooses this moment to show up. He doesn't shove through the bushes as usual, but comes down the driveway. Either he's grown up or— No. He just has his hands full and can't fit through bushes. He's carrying his fishing equipment and with difficulty is balancing something else as well. He sees the two men, he sees the Crown Vic, he sees Miranda on the porch and he pauses.

She wonders vaguely why his towel is still lying on the dock when he's coming from his house. It can't mean anything except that he forgot it when he headed home. Doesn't she have enough trouble without worrying about other people's towels?

"Who's this?" the police ask Miranda.

"Another neighbor. We let people who don't have their own docks use ours. Geoffrey likes to fish off our dock."

Geoffrey is wearing khaki shorts and a huge T-shirt, which makes him look even heavier. Miranda and Geoffrey are not Facebook friends, although Miranda generally wants to know everything about everybody and never turns down a friend request. I'm judging him by his extra pounds, thinks Miranda.

She has a sick, swampy vision of a life in which *she* is judged; judged as the sister of a murderer. A life in which she visits that murderer in prison. In which everybody will wonder what it's like to grow up with a murderer. In which Miranda carries this hideous truth through every hour of every class for two more years of high school.

"Are you okay, Rimmie?" asks Geoffrey. He sets his fishing gear carefully on the grass and straightens, throwing back his shoulders, as if willing to beat the police up should Miranda require this.

Normally she would be insulted. Of course she's okay. But this time she blinks away tears. "No. I'm not okay," she says, hoping this will touch the hearts of the detectives and they'll get in their car and leave.

Geoffrey comes forward with the other thing he has been holding. It's a platter of cookies. There is no wrapping over them. The scent of cinnamon is strong. "My mom made them for you," he says.

"Thank you," she says, but she is not thankful. Food is what you send for funerals. Geoffrey's mother must believe that Lander did it; that Lander is now a death in the family.

Geoffrey's mother has not brought the cookies herself,

because she doesn't know what to say. She's forcing poor Geoffrey, tongue-tied at the best of times, to do the talking.

Miranda does not have to hold the plate, because Henry and Hayden take it, biting into cookies they do not finish, then trying another one to see if the icing is thicker. Henry offers the police some cookies. "Take the bitten one," he says generously.

Geoffrey says to the detectives, "Are you here because of Lander?"

"Yes. What's your name, son?"

He spells his name. "Lander didn't do it," he says calmly.

His firm factual voice is reassuring. The detectives' skeptical nods are not. Miranda sits down hard, her knees buckling from anxiety.

The detectives say, "Geoffrey, why don't you sit here on the porch and keep Miranda company while we're inside?"

"Are they allowed to do that?" Geoffrey asks Miranda. "You think I should go get my dad?"

Geoffrey's father is yet another invisible parent. He too works in Hartford, but unlike Miranda's father (who during the school year commutes only two miles from the West Hartford house), Geoffrey's father commutes year-round from here. It's a hard drive in summer, and a brutal drive in winter. Geoffrey's mother is an interior decorator who works anywhere and everywhere. Geoffrey is usually alone.

"They are allowed," says Miranda. "Have a seat," she adds, desperate for Geoffrey to stay; desperate for allies.

Geoffrey sits. He's a very solid person. He completely

fills that chair. She tries to smile at him but her lips are quivering. He half reaches toward her, as if to pat her hand or her shoulder, but it isn't a gesture he's comfortable with, and the hand hangs there, not knowing what to do.

Me too, thinks Miranda, very close to sobbing. I have no idea what to do.

"Miranda," says one detective, "it turns out we took your iPad yesterday when we wanted Lander's."

"Oh," she says. "Is that what happened to my iPad? May I have it back please?" She can't even look at them. She is supposed to be the world's best exaggerator and she can't even fake innocence for five seconds. She looks at Geoffrey instead. He looks more alert than usual. Almost shocked.

Why? What is it to Geoffrey that the police do or don't have Lander's iPad?

"Miranda, where is Lander's iPad?" says the detective sharply.

"Don't yell at her," says Geoffrey just as sharply.

Is he protecting Miranda or the iPad? Does *Geoffrey* know something? What could *Geoffrey* know about Lander's situation?

Towels, she thinks. Rivers. Drugs.

"I don't know where Lander's iPad is," she says. This is a true statement, because Jack could have taken it anywhere, although it's a fairly safe bet that Jack has run up to his room, which is crowded with electronic devices, and is now working with Tanner on sending the entire world messages. *Find Jason Firenza.* She wonders how fast Tanner and

Jack work and what they have in mind, anyway, since her own mind is empty.

"Why was your iPad in Lander's room?" asks the detective.

"We share sometimes."

This is untrue. The sisters share approximately never. In fact, the white shirt with the lace sides may be the last thing they ever share. Miranda bursts into tears. When will she and Lander be real sisters? Ever? Probably not. They had their chances and blew them all. "What have you found out about Jason Firenza?" Miranda cries. "He really did it. I know you know that! You know Lander hasn't done anything!"

The detectives look at her gently and go into the house.

They can believe that Jason Firenza is the driver of the boat and the trafficker of drugs. But Lander is the killer.

Geoffrey coaxes Henry and Hayden to go home. Then he sits awkwardly on a rocking chair, not rocking, staring at the front yard.

Ants crawl up on the cookie plate.

"I brought the kayak back," he says.

What is he talking about? Miranda focuses on Geoffrey again. He has a large head: big jaw, big forehead, big amounts of hair. Now he shrugs a little. Big shoulders, too, she thinks.

"Lander paddled down to Two Willows to meet Jason," says Geoffrey. "That was on TV. So that meant your kayak was still at the marina. So I brought it back."

"Your parents drove you all the way and dropped you off and you paddled back?"

"No. I swam down."

"Two miles? And then across the whole river?"

"I do that all the time. I'm captain of my swim team."

Miranda sits in the terrible heat, overcome by how little she knows about anybody. Even Lander. Does she know a single thing that matters about her own sister?

Yes, she tells herself. *I know my sister is innocent.*

But Miranda does not know this.

The awful possibility of Lander's guilt wavers in her mind, like a heat mirage on a hot tar road.

7

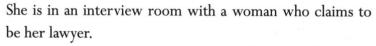

She is in an interview room with a woman who claims to be her lawyer.

The woman is heavy and lumpy. She wears a navy-blue suit in a fabric Lander would never put on her body. A tight knit shirt reveals rolls of fat. The lawyer wears no earrings, necklace or bracelet. Her watch has a leather band. Her hair is yanked back into a thin, graceless ponytail.

It is frightening. No kind, gentle attorney for a homicide case, but a woman who can't be bothered with frills. Because when you face prison, everything else is a frill.

The policewoman removes one cuff and fastens it to the chair. Lander brings her free hand to her face, reassuring herself that the hand still works.

The policewoman leaves them in private.

"Your parents retained me," says the lawyer.

My parents know I'm here.

Lander's pretense that this would go away in the night, that nobody would ever know, that she would walk away stained in heart but not in public, is destroyed.

Her parents, who spend their lives admiring her, displaying her, bragging about her—her parents know that she is in jail, accused of murder. They have found this criminal attorney. It is late Saturday afternoon. They found this woman at jet speed. Lander can't imagine her parents achieving this.

"How are they?" whispers Lander. She knows the answer. They are in the same shape Lander is in. *How can this be happening?* they are screaming silently. *Make it end! Make it go away!*

She struggles to breathe evenly.

The lawyer says, "Lander, you were brave and correct to say nothing to the police. That was a good decision. But I am your lawyer. You must talk to me or I cannot help you. We don't have much time because your parents cannot afford much time. I am expensive. Your parents are broke."

This is such an odd statement that fear gives way to annoyance. "Broke?" she echoes irritably.

"They are mortgaged to the hilt on both their houses. They have loans on both their cars. They have huge credit card debt. They have no savings. They have spent it all, my dear, on you. Your orthodontist, your riding lessons, your piano lessons, your clothes, your costly summer music camps in the Berkshires, your college, your ski weekends, your trips to Europe and now your medical school. But they don't have to worry about that particular payment because you are not going there."

Her father often says, *Kiddo, we can't do that. We don't have a dime.* Or, *Maybe next year. Right now I just barely have my head above water.*

It has never occurred to Lander that he means it. She has always thought of these as just little sayings, tossed out to stop a conversation.

Her parents have no money. Because of her.

"Listen up, Lander. A lot of what I'm telling you I got from television, Twitter or Facebook. People have been very cooperative with the media and very free online. First of all, two crew members on that barge and one person with riverfront property believe that Jason Firenza intentionally dropped his friend Derry Romaine into the water in front of the barge."

The very thing Miranda had said. A thing so dreadful that Lander considered it unthinkable, so she didn't think it. If only she had paid attention to her little sister. But does she ever pay attention to Rimmie?

Yet another burden of guilt to carry. Her failure as a sister.

And how, if Lander is confined behind bars, will they ever be close sisters?

"If so, it was an intended homicide," says the lawyer. "I'm not sure that killing via barge and water ski could be proved in a court, but it's an interesting detail, because a minute later, Jason Firenza was at your dock, drinking your coffee.

He did not participate in the search for his friend. Strangers saved the friend while Jason Firenza chatted with you. Think that doesn't creep people out? And the café at Two Willows Marina reports that you and Jason were laughing and flirting only a few hours later. You posted pictures of yourself and Jason on Facebook. None of the photographs predate the barge day, but your captions imply long-term friendship. So the assumption is that Jason Firenza was no stranger to your family in spite of claims to the contrary, and that you are probably part of the first attempt on Derry Romaine's life."

Lander tilts back in the chair, as if to avoid these terrible words. The wrist still chained to the chair catches painfully in the metal cuff.

She probably took a hundred pictures of Jason, and just as many selfies of the two of them laughing into her cell phone camera. She loved tilting her head and body close to his, so that they fit in the frame. In her hopes, Jason would fit into the frame of their lives together.

The frame of her life is now a jail cell.

"Derry Romaine disappeared from the hospital bed," says the lawyer. "He was not well enough to walk out on his own. A hospital desk clerk has identified Jason Firenza as a frequent visitor. It is likely that Jason Firenza got Derry Romaine out of the hospital, possibly with your assistance."

Lander never actually saw Derry Romaine. When he was rescued, emergency personnel made everybody leave the dock. By the time the stretcher was maneuvered up the cliff stairs, Lander was across the grass, listening to Jason answer the trooper's questions.

"Killing a colleague is not uncommon among drug dealers," says the lawyer. "The media speculates that when drowning him in the river didn't work, you two lured him down to that marsh, or carried him if he was that weak, and shot him in the back."

Lander's body is nodding and jittering as if she is some ancient, pathetic creature with palsy. "No! Nothing like that happened." But how else could Derry Romaine have arrived in that grim little woods except by Jason bringing him there?

She imagines Jason sneaking Derry into those woods. But however Derry got there, it couldn't have been Jason, because Jason was with her.

In her imagination, she sees the gun in her hand. She sees the bullet leave the gun. She sees it hit Derry, puncture his flesh, explode in his chest. She sees the poor boy's body as it contorts, convulses, collapses.

It is so real that Lander wonders if she *has* seen this. If she knew at the time what she was doing. If she *is* a murderer.

The lawyer says, "I'm quoting the media. That's their story and a large amount is not fact. For example, one TV station claims that your fingerprints are the only ones on the murder weapon. But it's the weekend. Labs don't work that fast. The gun you held is not yet proven to be the murder weapon and neither has it been fingerprinted. Now tell me your story."

Lander closes her eyes tight to squash the vision of

Derry Romaine dying from her bullet. Could it have been some *other* gun that did it? But there is no other gun and nobody else was shooting.

"Have you arranged bail yet?" she whispers. She is quoting television shows. People are always getting out on bail. There are entire companies whose sole purpose is to provide bail. Even if you're broke—she has a hard time accepting that her family is broke—they figure out a way to fund bail for you.

"You're accused of homicide, Lander. A judge isn't likely to give you bail."

"I can't stay here!"

"Pull yourself together, Lander. You are twenty-two years old. You are in trouble, and you aren't going anywhere. The facts are grim. Talk to me."

You aren't going anywhere.

Lander's entire life is about freedom. She has always gone anywhere. To the top of the class. To the mall. To Europe. To ski resorts.

She tries not to be a crybaby, but the only thing she wants to do is fling herself facedown on her own bed and bawl, something she has not done since middle school. She swallows hard and finds her voice. "Can my parents be here while I talk to you?"

The lawyer stares incredulously. "I've heard of helicopter parents, how they go to college interviews with their children. How they even show up at the kid's job interviews. But they don't share jail, Lander. You get a prison term, it's *your* prison term."

STILL SATURDAY

Her parents text Miranda on and off all day. The attorney recommended by several West Hartford people is already visiting the jail. Her father in his car has driven down to the shoreline to wait with her mother. They want to be together and are befuddled by having an extra car. They want to see their daughter and can't.

They do not use Lander's name. They say "she" or "her." They cannot attach that precious name to this nightmare.

Miranda receives two casseroles and a basket of big red homegrown tomatoes. The neighbors time delivery to avoid Miranda's parents. They scoot over fast and leave soon. "Miranda, darling. We know this misunderstanding will be cleared up." "Miranda, honey, you tell your mom and dad to call if we can do anything." "Are you all right, Rimmie? Do you want me to stay for a while?"

Like her parents, the neighbors do not use the word "Lander." The name has become taboo. The whole situation is taboo. Nobody actually refers to it.

Miranda rearranges the entire refrigerator to get the casseroles in. Why do casseroles come in such huge, thick ceramic containers? Nobody will eat this stuff. The Allerdons are a family in love with food, but if they can swallow anything tonight, it won't be somebody else's tuna fish.

The living room is in a state of squalor. Abandoned food, dirty plates, empty juice boxes, little boys' socks, Barrel's dog hair floating in the shafts of sunlight, pillows on the floor, afghan used for a tent.

Miranda tells Henry and Hayden to go home, or she will have to lock them in Barrel's run. They love this, and race out the front door and lock themselves in Barrel's run, where they bark happily. Barrel will growl on demand, but he is not a barker, even in the wild excitement of company in his run.

Miranda cleans like a tornado, spinning from room to room. She runs the electric broom, Swiffers the bare wood floors, Dustbusters the crumb-covered sofa.

In the kitchen she wants to give up. The dishwasher is full of clean dishes while the small counter and single sink are heaped with dirty ones. The task of emptying and refilling seems utterly beyond her ability.

She takes out the plastic basket of clean silverware and is sobbing before the spoons are in their proper places.

What does it matter if the cottage is tidy? Their lives are ruined. No one cares about dust.

Somebody clears his throat.

Miranda drops the silver and crashes painfully against the counter. There in the porch doorway is Stu, holding yet another casserole.

Nobody's dead yet, she thinks. Stop bringing these casseroles! Then she remembers that this is not true: Derry Romaine is dead.

Stu is staring at her, bright-eyed as a squirrel. Miranda hates squirrels. One year, when Miranda accidentally left the open birdseed bag out on the porch, squirrels chewed right through the screens to get at the seed they smelled. The Allerdons came home to rodent-destroyed pillows and six windows that had to be repaired.

Stu's not a squirrel, she tells herself. *He's perfectly decent-looking. Even Lander went out with him and she has very high standards.*

Of course, Lander refused to go out a second time, so maybe Stu is a squirrel.

"Here. I'll put it all away," says Stu. "You sit on the stool and tell me what's happening. You look awful, by the way."

Just how this should be a comfort is not clear.

"How is Lander doing?" Stu asks.

The neighborhood boys are the only people to use Lander's name. What does this mean?

Miranda sits on the stool. The kitchen is too small for two stools. There is a narrow knee hole so that one slim person can have one small meal on the short stretch of counter.

Sell the cottage, she remembers. The mere thought makes her dizzy; makes it difficult to put her mind on anything else.

Stu opens the refrigerator to slide his casserole in, and laughs. "You'll have to eat ours first," he says, "because there's no room in here."

What is there to laugh about? Miranda is shaking with dislike. She wants to say "Please thank your mother for me," but Mrs. Crowder hasn't come herself. She has sent her son. Mrs. Crowder can mix canned soup with macaroni, but she can't say "I know Lander is innocent."

Nobody is saying that Lander is innocent.

Not even their own parents. Not Jack. Not Stu.

Wait. Geoffrey is. Why is Geoffrey sure? Why am I sure?

What do the rest of them know about my sister that they think she really could kill somebody?

Miranda's body aches, as if her heart can't take it anymore and is transferring the pain to her bones.

Stu says, "The dinner plates?"

Miranda feels as if she has a new specialty: gaping stupidly at people who ask meaningless questions.

"I don't know where they go," explains Stu.

Miranda pulls herself together and points to the right shelf. Stu stacks crockery. "Seriously," he says, "how is

Lander doing?" He deposits a frown on his forehead. The frown is a total fake.

Miranda frowns back. "I don't know. I suppose she's doing awful."

"Are your folks visiting her?" Now he's nodding, because he expects the answer to be yes.

"They haven't seen her yet. I think the police are still processing her."

"Processing," echoes Stu. He takes his frown off. "There's a word. What does it mean? Putting her through some kind of wringer?"

"I suppose. Fingerprints, maybe? Jail uniform? I don't know, Stu. I can't even picture it because it's Lander. How could it be *Lander* going through this?"

"Even Lander may not be strong enough for this," agrees Stu. Now the real Stu shows up on his face. He's like the TV anchors. He is fascinated. He yearns for details. Miranda hides behind the dish towel to keep from spitting on him.

"Are you the one putting the photographs and videos out there?" he asks. "It's pretty clever, using Lander's Facebook page. And her Twitter."

What good does it do anybody to be clever? Lander is the cleverest person they've ever known, and look where she is. Jack and Tanner are clever, too, but clever isn't going to rescue Lander.

Her cell phone signals yet another message. The phone is full of unread messages. All her friends have texted and probably if she were to go to her own Facebook page, she would find a hundred posts. But Miranda's heart and mind are limited. She can't waste time on her own friends. It's Lander's friends and acquaintances she has to search.

With the absolute last shred of poise that Miranda possesses, she says, "Thank you so much for your help, Stu." She means "Get out of here," but he's too dim to understand.

"Rimmie." He leans toward her, too close. But it's a tiny kitchen. Everybody is too close there. "Rimmie, I want a phone call the minute you've talked to Lander."

She nods. But she will not call him. She won't call anybody. And if she texts somebody, Stu is maybe the millionth possibility. She gives his arm a tiny push and he reluctantly steps out onto the screened porch. "You sure you're okay on your own?" he asks. The sun is in his eyes. He squints and now he looks like an ogre instead of a squirrel.

"I'm fine," she says, although she plans to bury her face in her pillow and sob because all the neighbors have turned out to be ogres.

"I could help you with the online stuff. It's my gig, you know. Computers."

She attaches a polite negative smile to her face, shakes her head and closes the door on Stu.

When she is absolutely sure Stu is gone, she goes out onto the screened porch and latches both its side doors. She reenters the cottage and not only latches the kitchen and living room doors to the porch, but also bolts the inner solid-wood doors. In her bedroom, she lowers the window that opens onto the porch and is crucial for cross-ventilation, and locks it.

She bolts the front door.

It was suffocatingly hot in the cottage already. Now it's even hotter. For the first time in her life, Miranda hates the cottage. She goes into the tiny bathroom she and Lander share—the bathroom with no trace of either sister. Whichever neighborhood boy used it last made a mess. She hates whoever it is. She hates all of them. She hates everything.

In the only room with no windows, the only place that feels protected, Miranda breaks down. Sobs rise from her chest like howls from a wolf.

It is dark by the time her parents get home. Miranda is desperately glad to see them. The cottage is no longer vacant and shadowy. It is warm with family. "How is Lander doing?" she cries. "Could you give her a hug? What did she tell you?"

It turns out that visiting a person charged with homicide is not a right. A parent can't just walk into the jail and see her daughter. The police think that tomorrow, Sunday, the Allerdons can see Lander.

Miranda's parents put their arms around her, but their grip is flaccid. They are utterly without strength.

Miranda gets her father a Coke and her mother a Sprite. They drink deeply, as if they haven't had liquid in days.

They describe their efforts. All day, on their cell phones, they swallowed their pride and called relatives, begging for money. An adult cousin actually laughed, thinking the murder story was a sick, off-the-wall joke. *Lander?* Come on.

The cousin offered a hundred dollars, a sum that is meaningless in the face of what the attorney charges, but Miranda's parents were forced to say *Thank you, you are so kind.*

Finally, Miranda's grandmother, her father's mother, pledged her house. Grandma has an open line of credit she has never used. She will write a check for whatever her son and daughter-in-law need.

Miranda's grandmother is elderly and in poor health. An aide does housework and drives her on errands, because Grandma can no longer see well enough to drive. She depends on friends and church family to take her everywhere once the aide leaves. The aide is paid through medical insurance. Grandma lives very frugally in order to stay in the house she's loved for fifty years.

Grandma has absolutely no way to repay a loan.

Miranda's parents are sick with gratitude that money has been found and sicker with fear. How will they repay Grandma? If they don't pay her back, she'll lose the house.

Miranda tries not to think of her own future, when Lander's is so bleak. But she can't help it. Her parents have spent all they have and more; they are in debt for Lander's college, which is over, and for the first year of medical school—a bill they have had to pay even though medical school hasn't started.

There isn't money for Miranda to go to college.

There never was, even without attorneys' bills.

Either her parents tell themselves that somehow they'll make it work for daughter number two, or they shrug about daughter number two. In every way, Lander is always daughter number one.

Now they are arguing about whether to call the medical school Monday morning and ask to have the tuition returned. This would be a lot of cash, but it means telling the admissions department why Lander will not be attending.

"No," says Miranda's mother. "She'll still go to medical school. This will work out somehow. We can't crush her future by exploding this—this *thing*—so early."

Lander's future is already crushed.

It is crushed by her poor judgment, dating Jason Firenza, even though she witnessed his callous stupidity.

It is crushed by her poor judgment, choosing to play with guns.

And perhaps crushed by her decision—the only explanation Miranda can think of—to protect Jason. Surely it was Jason who put a bullet in Derry Romaine. And then Lander wiped the gun, removed Jason's prints and put her own there.

Miranda cannot get within miles of such an insane decision. Particularly such an insane decision on the part of the smartest person she knows.

Miranda and her parents migrate to the porch and sit

staring at the river. In the dark it is sleek and mysterious. Water pats the riverbank like the footsteps of strangers approaching.

Miranda doesn't even bother to take the lid off Mrs. Crowder's casserole and see what's in there. She cuts up a few of the fine red garden tomatoes, sprinkles olive oil and salt on them, brings them back with forks and hunks of bakery bread.

Nobody touches anything.

"Tell me about the lawyer," Miranda says.

The lawyer is solid, stodgy, experienced. She does not smile. She offers no comfort to these terrified parents. She will do what she can "to mitigate the seriousness of Lander's situation."

Does this mean Lander's own lawyer is not trying to prove Lander's innocence? Just trying to make Lander's guilt less serious?

In the sweltering evening, Miranda's hands ice up. "Has Lander explained that it was an accident? Or self-defense?"

Her father's face is trembling. She has never seen this before. One cheek quivers differently from the other, as if he is developing a dimple there, or having a stroke. He shrugs, because he can come up with no other motion. "I guess she hasn't said much of anything."

Candy telephones.

Miranda stares at the caller ID of her dearest friend. She doesn't answer. Her head thunders. She takes a few aspirin and spends Saturday night on the porch, sleeping fitfully on the chaise longue in its flat position. Every now and then she reads the news banners on her phone. There are interviews with "experts." Nobody seems to have facts, but they're eager to present guesses. A retired cop discusses drug dealing along the river. Drug dealing is a young man's game, the experienced cop says. As he talks, the screen displays a photo of Lander and Jason probably taken off her Facebook. It looks like a selfie. The implication is that Jason—a young man—and Lander, his girlfriend, are drug dealers.

SUNDAY MORNING

At dawn, it is drizzling, which does not stop the bass fishermen, who continually zoom downriver. A few boats fish at
the water's edge below the Allerdons' bluff. It's a good spot,
because several feet below the surface of the water is a jut-
ting shelf of bedrock, and fish like it there. Miranda cannot
see the men, but is forced to listen to them talk. It is not the
usual fishermen's talk, which is boring and confined to fish.

"What do you think?" The voice is excited.

"Yep. It's this house. I checked Google Maps for Allerdon, and theirs is the only one right at the water's edge."

"Did you see the barge thing happen?"

"No, but there are two videos on YouTube. Neither one
actually shows the guy getting sucked under, though," says
the voice regretfully.

These men are not fishing. They are sight-seeing. *This is where the murderer lives! This is where she met her boyfriend!*

When they motor away, Miranda slips outside, barefoot on the dewy grass, and fastens the gate at the top of the cliff stairs. It's not a security lock, just a safety lock. Anybody could open it by feeling around the backside of the gate. Miranda pretends that it will hold off trespassers.

Back inside, Miranda realizes that today is Sunday.

Here at the cottage, they attend summer church. It's a lovely small white clapboard church way out in the country, high on a grassy hill, open only in July and August. A retired minister who lives nearby officiates, and a pianist plays the hymns.

Summer church is airy, with the doors left open, and tall, thin windows framing green leaves and blue sky. Summer church is as much a part of their cottage world as the river. Miranda wonders what hymns they will sing this morning. Lander, who is a brilliant pianist, often plays the prelude. They probably don't have grand pianos in prison.

Miranda and her parents toy with breakfast. Dishes are soiled, but nothing is eaten. Coffee is made, but mugs are untouched.

Although church is their source of comfort, worship and friendship, they cannot face all those people. To be the object of pity and prayer is appalling. They skip church.

Around nine, her parents leave. They will drive south to the shoreline and the jail where Lander is sitting. They will camp in the waiting room. They are desperate to see her. Desperate to meet again with the lawyer.

Desperate.

They ask if Miranda wishes to come but she doesn't. It's not a family outing. And again today, she is possessed by the sensation that if she just formulates the right plan, she will find Jason. He *has* to be the killer!

But she has no plan.

Barrel's owners come over.

Both the Nevilles are doctors. They practice in Hartford, and do not frequently get down to their weekend place. They have a live-in housekeeper, whom Miranda never sees except when the woman fills Barrel's bowl. In Miranda's opinion, the Nevilles have a dog solely to bolster their persona as the kind of people who rescue dogs.

Their slim, trim bodies are clad in matching silver-and-green running outfits and they are dancing on their very expensive running shoes, preparatory to the sort of five-mile jaunt they like.

"Miranda, darling," says Dr. Neville the wife. "We are horrified. How can we help?"

They probably *are* horrified, but if they really wanted to help, they'd have come over before her parents drove away.

Perhaps Miranda should ask for money. The doctors surely have tons of it.

"How is your poor sister doing?" they ask.

Miranda does not know how Lander is doing.

Is Lander confessing strings of wild sentences explaining how she came to be a murderer? Sitting quietly, mentally running through the chemistry formulas she will need in medical school? Making friends with other female prisoners, perhaps helping them to prepare a defense? Pounding her fists on a barred door, screaming for release?

"We're going out for breakfast after our run," says Dr. Neville the husband. "Would you like to come with us?"

The Nevilles have no interest in the neighborhood and do not participate in the barbecues, picnics and celebrations that her parents so often host.

Why do they even have this house when they are so rarely here? Who really is that housekeeper who is not just invisible but also afraid of Barrel? Why do they have Barrel? Why do they suddenly want Miranda's company?

Jason Firenza must deal drugs, because that package of cocaine must be his. To whom does he deliver?

It seems to her that the entire neighborhood is packed with people who could be part of this; who could be the reason Jason is ever on this stretch of the river to start with.

Right there, while they jog in place, she checks the Nevilles' Facebook page on her cell.

They have one of those blank snooty pages, without even a photograph of either one of them. They do of course list the colleges they attended, which are famous and important.

Even if she sends a friend request to these doctors so that she can see what they've really posted, they probably work eighteen-hour days and won't notice until next week.

"That's so nice of you," she says. "But I have phone calls to make."

She will start with Willow, Lander's best friend. What has Lander told Willow?

"Mir-an-da!" cries Willow, and in those three stretched-out syllables Miranda knows this is not good. "Miranda, how *are* you? You poor, poor *thing*. I've been so *worried* about you."

Shouldn't Willow be worried about Lander? "Willow, did you talk to Lander this week?"

"A couple times. She is madly in love with this guy, you know. Jason this, Jason that. I mean, Lander is skeptical of men. And for her to fall so hard. I wanted to laugh. But of course I was very, very supportive and asked when we all could get together."

Henry and Hayden arrive. "Don't worry, we brought our own breakfast," they tell Miranda, shaking a box of sugar cereal and holding up a quart of milk.

Are Mr. and Mrs. Warren happy to have a break from their sons? Or do they want a break from witnesses? The Warren property is far and away the most private on the river side of the road, because to their north is that deep ravine. Nobody can see anything that happens in the Warrens' backyard. On the other hand, they do not have dock rights. A boat cannot tie up along their property.

Miranda has no reason to suspect a single person in her neighborhood of drug trafficking. I'm just so desperate, she thinks. I'll shove Lander's guilt off on anybody. She slogs on through her phone call. "I need your help, Willow." Her voice squeals like a bad hinge. "I need you to tell me everything Lander said about Jason Firenza."

"She said he was perfect and romantic and thoughtful and funny and adorable. I mean, I knew from the beginning she would kill for this guy."

Miranda gasps.

"I'm sorry!" cries Willow. "Of course I didn't mean that. It's just a phrase. Of course you and I know that Lander is a fine person, a moral person, a good person, and yet the facts look very bad, Rimmie, and we have to face the facts. Even a fine, fine person can have a moment of rage or whatever."

Miranda hates Willow. Hates her so passionately she could stab the woman. This is how murder happens. Willow is lucky she's in West Hartford. Miranda grits her teeth. "Forget that," she says to Willow. "We have to identify Jason Firenza."

"Somebody has. You haven't looked at Facebook in a few hours. He's a person named Jason Draft."

Miranda disconnects. Her interest in Willow is permanently over.

Jack still has her iPad. She texts. Come over. Bring iPad.

He texts back. Dad's taking me to a ball game in Norwich.

She texts. Either be too sick to go or bring me the iPad first.

The knock on the front door is immediate and she whirls around, startled. It's Stu, waving a white paper bakery bag. Wasn't he just here? Didn't she just get rid of him? Or was that yesterday? How many weeks have passed since the police arrived at their door? Or is it only hours? Why does Stu care more than Willow? Why aren't Miranda's parents here to hold her tight? Why did Lander go anywhere, ever, with Jason Firenza?

Henry and Hayden attack Stu. "What did you bring? Can we have some?" Really, they're a little pack of canines.

Stu lifts the white bag out of the boys' reach. "Donuts. For Rimmie. Sugar solves so many problems."

Stu is an idiot. Sugar won't solve a thing. Finding Jason Firenza, also known as Jason Draft, might.

Stu drops into a wicker chair, as if planning to stay; as if he might ask for coffee next. Or worse, want to know if everybody enjoyed his mother's casserole.

Stu offers Miranda a donut but she shakes her head.

"How is Lander?" asks Stu. "I'm so worried. Do they have her in with violent criminals and stuff?"

It has not occurred to Miranda that there will be other prisoners. She pictures vicious women circling her sister, making knives out of plastic plates and stabbing her. She has to get Lander out of there! She has to find Jason Firenza. She wants the iPad back from Jack. She doesn't need Stu or the little boys noticing. She texts Jack again. Hide it under your jacket.

And now here's Geoffrey! Is it always like this? Do

neighborhood boys crawl out from under the shrubbery on normal summer days? Or have they synchronized their watches and decided to do this on purpose to tip Miranda over the brink into insanity? Not that anyone wears a watch.

They just want to be part of the action, she thinks. If only there were action here! I am the symbol of non-action. I'm staring at rocking chairs when I should be rescuing my sister from jail.

Geoffrey approaches awkwardly. He doesn't quite look at Stu and he doesn't quite look at Miranda. "Hi," he says. "You weren't in church this morning."

Stu looks as if he might laugh.

"We prayed for you," says Geoffrey. He flushes. Prayer is intense; private; hard to bring up. She wants to be grateful but she is simply more horrified. The whole congregation knows. Pretty soon she'll have even more casseroles.

At last Jack texts back. What jacket? It's 86 out.

Miranda is desperate to be alone with that iPad. She wants Stu and Geoffrey to leave. She wants Jack.

Yet another car comes down the driveway. It is the minister from summer church.

He's quite elderly, having been retired for decades, but he loves the eight weeks each year when he has his vocation back. He gets out of the car and simply holds out his arms to Miranda.

Miranda, whose parents are too shocked to offer comfort, cries against the soft fabric of his shirt. There is nothing like a loving grown-up. When she stops crying, he gives her a real cotton handkerchief, snowy white and ironed. She mops her face.

Stu is gone. Geoffrey is gone. The little boys are playing in their tree house.

Well, now she knows how to empty the place: call in the clergy.

The minister says gently, "Your mother and father?"

"At the jail. Hoping to visit Lander. They haven't been allowed to yet."

The minister looks somber. Under the circumstances, how else could he look?

"Miranda, my grandson is worried about you. I do not understand much about Facebook and Twitter and so forth, but my grandson came to summer church this morning hoping to see your family. He says you are advertising for a murderer. And that murderer is out here somewhere."

Miranda is joyful. "You believe Lander didn't do it?"

"I've known Lander all her life. She is not a killer. But I suspect she has made dreadful decisions. I don't want you making equally dreadful decisions. Staying alone would be one of those. We are dealing with a killer and you are letting him know that you are hunting for him." But Miranda is hunting online and is herself invisible and unnamed. She is not alarmed.

Jack arrives. He is wearing jeans, a T-shirt and bright floppy sneakers without socks. A small backpack hangs from one strap on his shoulder. The iPad must be in the backpack.

In his hands is some huge concoction. When he is closer, she sees that it is a fruit arrangement: the kind where they carve cantaloupe into daisies and put them on sticks in a watermelon basket. Jack is fending off bees and wasps that want some of the sweet juice.

With the minister holding the front door open and waving the bees off, Jack scoots in first, then Miranda, and then the minister.

One bee gets in. Jack carefully deposits his fruit bouquet on the coffee table, lets his backpack slip to the floor, picks up a magazine and efficiently swats the bee. He beams proudly. He doesn't pick up the dead bee.

The minister repeats his statement that Miranda must not be here alone. "We are talking about drug traffickers who shoot each other. I want to be sure that you are safely among friends, Miranda. Now. Have you had dinner? My wife and grandson and I would love to take you to dinner."

Sunday is the only midday meal referred to as dinner. Miranda hasn't eaten since yesterday. She loves the minister, who is on her team, and she loves his grandson, of whom she has never heard and who could be sixteen or forty, and she loves his wife, a pretty lady now deep in dementia, who has retained nothing but her beautiful smile.

There is no question about dinner, however. Miranda must stay here and stay focused. She has to read up on Jason Draft. She will fib, and say that her good friend Candy's family is driving down to get her.

Jack has a better move. "She's coming to the ball game with us. It's in Norwich. Have you ever been to that stadium?"

"I have," says the minister, smiling. "I love baseball. This is perfect, Miranda. It will take your mind off a situation you cannot change."

I can change it, thinks Miranda. I have to change it.

"I will stop worrying," says the minister, giving her a last hug. He gets into his car. "And I will keep praying," he promises.

When he is out of sight, Jack says, "I think you should come to the ball game."

She shakes her head. She is probably the only person in the whole world who hasn't yet seen the posts on Jason Draft. And she has to check out the rest of the neighborhood. She's done only the Nevilles and the Warrens.

Jack says hopefully, "Do you think he's right? Do you think drug traffickers and killers are hanging around right now?"

"I think they're done killing," says Miranda. But is anybody ever *done* with drug dealing? Isn't it always going on?

Jack is reluctant to leave, even for a great baseball game. Or a bad one, which is often the case in the minor leagues. "Keep texting," he says. "I want to know everything."

"If we knew everything," says Miranda, "we would be getting Lander out of jail."

Jack gives her a funny look, and she realizes that he does not expect Lander to get out of jail at all.

8

This time when the detectives question Lander, the lawyer will be with her.

The police will ask questions she isn't going to answer and the lawyer will tell her not to anyway.

She drags herself down the hall. She is so tired she could sleep for a week.

The lawyer says it is Sunday.

Day of rest. Day of worship. Day of thick heavy newspapers.

She is religious. But she cannot pray. If she has shot a man in the back, she cannot face God. God forgives the person who repents, but he also knows that Lander fakes repentance. Lander's usual sins are brushing somebody off, speaking sharply to somebody she thinks is stupid or ignoring somebody when she knows perfectly well they're there. She does it constantly, knowing she's being ugly, but enjoying herself. It's fun being superior. On Sunday, routinely, she repents, knowing she'll behave the same way next week.

Today it is possible that her sin is murder.

God knows. Perhaps Jason knows. But Lander still does not know.

She is desperate to get her mind on something else. She throws her thoughts toward summer visitors, summer days, summer church. During that boring date with Stu, he laughed at her for attending church. *"Weed,"* he had said, *"does the job just as well."*

"Just as well as what?" Lander had asked.

"All that prayer stuff. Smoke a little weed, Lanny, and you'll drift off into heaven. Plus, weed is more portable than church. And it never judges you."

Lander got to her feet then, saying, *"Stu, I have better things to do with my time than listen to somebody whose only skill is getting high."*

"Come on, Lanny, loosen up. Let's go to the movies tomorrow."

"I don't loosen," Lander had said, grateful that she had driven her father's car to meet Stu and was not depending on him for a ride home. She left him sitting at the table.

I don't loosen, thinks Lander now. But do I murder? Dear God, have I been priding myself on stupid things like never loosening up when in fact I kill people?

God, please don't let me be a killer.

Please let my parents visit.

Please don't let them ask if I did it.

If I did fire the shot that killed Derry Romaine, I didn't know, she tells herself. *Murder is less murderous if you didn't mean to.*

Or is it? Certainly not to the dead man.

She gags.

"Stop it," snaps the policeman. "Just stop it."

But out it comes, nothing but drool this time, a guilty little puddle on the floor.

She is now wearing jail clothing. It resembles the hospital scrubs she has worn for every volunteer position since her sixteenth birthday, throwing herself into medical work at any level, just to be there; to breathe in the excitement and speed and action of medicine.

Except that printed in block letters on the back of the shirt she wears now is the name of the jail. She can feel the letters against her bare skin. She's a cow, branded.

Stop it! she yells at herself. *You cannot feel the letters against your skin. They are printed on the outside of the fabric.*

Lander has always told people that clothing is of little interest to her; she is above fashion. But of course this is not true. She loves style. She believes she has achieved that classic look of effortless perfection.

Jail clothes are pretty effortless. But perfect? She thinks of her beautiful future, her success as a doctor, her life in some great city, her renown as a scientist. It's a mirage. She will be nothing but a felon.

Lander cannot let herself sink into self-pity. She must

consider every detail of Friday morning. There is an explanation. She just has to find it. She closes her eyes and steps back into Friday.

As Jason arranges, on Friday morning, Lander paddles down to Two Willows Marina in her kayak. He is waiting on the dock, grinning and waving. They get into a car. It is his father's, Jason tells her, not his style.

Lander is not interested in cars and does not have one herself, either. She gives it no thought that an adult is borrowing his father's car.

Was it his father's car? she wonders now. Or stolen, like the boat?

She and Jason drive down Route 9, the north-south parkway on the west side of the Connecticut River. There's no such road on the east, where the cottage is. The land on the east is too rough, chopped up by marshes, massive rock outcrops and creeks.

Jason drove across the river where it meets Long Island Sound on the I-95 bridge and took the first exit. They were surrounded by pretty white houses and pretty green lawns, pretty tawny marsh grass and pretty seabirds floating in a pretty sky.

Jason is saying that his hobby is danger. As if anybody around here knows anything about danger. This zip code is all about ease and safety.

He loves doing things on the edge, he tells her. He loves when his pulse races, his heart rips and his nightmares deepen.

At the time, this sounds like movie dialogue. Now she

wonders if Jason was simply telling the truth. If part of his flirtation with danger was to tell Lander right up front that she too was in danger.

Jason turns into a marina she has never noticed. Anchored in a small private bay were breathtakingly beautiful yachts. Docked is an immense cruiser, which probably requires a crew of half a dozen, plus a chef.

She and Jason saunter around. When he smiles at her, Lander feels like a million dollars; a yacht owner has nothing on her.

A few people are being motored out to their boats by the marina attendant. But on a Friday morning, there is not much other activity. Jason helps her into a small motorboat with a console for the driver, a second comfy seat, a storage locker and no head. Lander's main thought is how she will pee. She believes this is why most boaters are men. They don't care about a flush toilet in a separate room with a door.

She says, "This isn't the *Paid at Last*."

"It's the *Water Fever*," he replies. "It belongs to a friend. I use it all the time." They putter out of the marina, weaving slowly among the yachts.

The police say that she and Jason steal this motorboat.

When they stroll around, is Jason looking for the right boat to steal? Does he know already which one he wants and is just waiting for the moment nobody is looking? Has he stolen that very boat before and then just returned it, so that it was stealing but also borrowing?

A large percentage of pleasure boats never leave their

marina. They are just inexpensive weekend places, the cost of docking a boat being a lot cheaper than buying waterfront. Boats are not cars. They are not used every day, ten times a day. They are not used when the owners are at work or when there are lightning storms. Mainly, boats sit and wait.

Does Jason keep track of which boats are never used? Does he know which owner never comes on a Friday? Or is he simply betting that the odds are in favor of the casual thief with the beautiful girlfriend?

Why steal a boat at all? Why not just own one? If he is dealing drugs on a large scale, he can certainly afford a boat. Or does stealing a boat satisfy Jason's zest for danger?

But the danger for a drug dealer is not the boat. It's the jail sentence. She knows now that jail is shame, isolation, fear, stench, boredom. Risk all that just to motor up and down a river for a few hours?

And there are other risks. Delivering the cocaine, for one. Is the package already in the *Water Fever* when she and Jason take it? Or does Jason bring the package with him? He has binoculars, hanging in a case around his neck. Is that case in fact full of drugs?

But the only reason to deal drugs is to make money. Why then did Jason abandon the package and leave her standing there to be found with it?

And there is of course the final risk. Death. Being shot, like Derry.

But Lander has these thoughts far too late. She is not thinking about anything except Jason when they head upstream in the *Water Fever,* completing the pointless circle by boat. But she says nothing because who cares? Lander cares only that Jason wanted her company.

Back in high school, back in the college dorm and the cafeteria, the classrooms and the labs, guys are always glad to see Lander. They do not ask her for dates. They simply assume that she will hang out where they hung out.

Is she in love with Jason for the simple pathetic reason that he singles her out? That he doesn't want a crowd; he wants her?

Lander thinks of herself as supremely confident. But if this is why she falls for Jason, she has no self-confidence at all.

In the jail corridor, she stops walking. She understands now why Jason arranges for her to kayak across the river to meet him Friday morning: because it is a slow method of travel. Followed by a forty-five-minute drive around the mouth of the river and a second little boat. *Jason is killing time.*

Killing time. So that they could then kill a man?

Jason motors behind one of the marshy islets that crowd the eastern bank of the Connecticut above its wide mouth. The waters are shallow. Jason finds a narrow channel winding through tall grass. Lander feels like an egret in an unexpected wilderness.

Now she thinks Jason was waiting for high tide. It would be impossible to reach that little woods at low tide, when the channel would be a trickle.

In the thready little creek, they go too slowly to make their own breeze. She is sweating and thirsty. They arrive at a low-lying woody swamp. It is not pretty. She is assuming they will do something delightful. Picnic, perhaps. It is lunchtime. She is vaguely aware that there is no food in the boat. Not even bottled water. But all their dining so far has been in restaurants. Perhaps this is the back way to some delightful country inn.

Jason is talking about hunting, which he loves. He always has a gun with him, he explains, in case there's a chance to hunt. She is repelled and he teases her, saying that she's missing one of the great hobbies of life.

Jason motors as close to the shore as he can. There are a few big flat stones, and behind them a profusion of vines, wildflowers and poison ivy. He steps off the boat, drags it onto the mud and gives Lander a hand out. She steps on one of the big stones and leaps to dry land.

"Wait here," he says. He walks into the woods and ties his bandanna about chin level on a slender sapling. She is so dopey with love for this man that she actually envies the tree; she would have liked Jason to tie that precious bandanna on her. When Jason turns and comes back, she cannot erase her smile.

Jason explains how to hold the gun.

At what point does she agree to try it?

The gun fits her palm. She doesn't need two hands, the way they do for a rifle on TV. The word "rifle" briefly penetrates her mind as she stands beside him, aiming at the bandanna. Don't people hunt with rifles? Or shotguns? Do they really hunt with whatever this is, a revolver or a pistol?

Jason does not put his own hand on that gun. In fact, the gun is produced lying in a special box, with a hinged lid. He holds out the box and tells her to pick the gun up and not be afraid of it. But he does not touch it himself.

So many clues. So many warnings. Lander ignores them all. She is not thinking in terms of warnings. She is thinking how much she likes Jason's company.

"Get going, Miss Allerdon!" barks the guard.

She has almost forgotten she is in jail. Her entire mind is standing in those woods.

When the police walk her out of the woods, there is a driveway. Whose house? What road does it connect to? When she is shoved into the back of the police car, she is too terrified to think of scenery and geography.

But the little wood is not far north of the interstate. I-95 is the conduit for all the drug traffic on the entire East Coast. Traffickers have to leave the highway to make their deliveries. Does Jason know this driveway well? Along with scoping out good boats to steal, does he scope out potential delivery sites?

It's a ghastly vision: people who peddle crack and coke and crystal meth, driving down every driveway, examining every garage, exploring every little branch of every little river. Looking for the place that is sufficiently isolated so that they can make unseen deliveries.

But why include Lander? It surely adds risk. Okay, Jason likes risk. But then why does he waste six days on dating her?

She admits to herself that only Jason could have tipped off the police. But why do it?

Why not let Derry's body lie there? As the tides came in and out, the body would have been consumed by land, sky and sea predators. It could have been years before the remains were found. It could have been never.

Her guard stops. There's a sign on a door. INTERVIEW ROOM.

"Interview" is a soft word. A word for the college admissions office or getting a job. This is an interview for prison.

It comes to her at last that a third person must have been involved. The circular motion across, down and around the river gives this other person time to set up Derry Romaine's murder. How could that person be sure that Lander will aim right? That Derry will stand there, waiting?

Furthermore, the only way Jason could vanish after the target practice is for that other person to wait up on the road with a car, or down in the marsh with another boat.

But who?

And why?

And why Lander?

Does somebody hate her enough to arrange a murder that would, as a by-product, also destroy her?

I am the most conceited person on earth, she thinks, staring at the vacant chair that is meant for her. I can actually pretend the murder of Derry Romaine happens because I am important.

SUNDAY AFTERNOON

With every visitor gone, Miranda is at last looking down at a screen that shows the real Jason Firenza: Jason Draft.

Whatever he calls himself, he's way too attractive to be a criminal.

The sofa is so soft and she is so tired. Her eyes burn with exhaustion. If she closes her eyes, she's done. Miranda stands up to prevent herself from napping.

Her next step is Jason Draft's Facebook page. She will study all his friends. A guy as handsome, aggressive and cocky as Jason will not bother with privacy controls because he will want everybody to admire him. Perhaps she will recognize a friend of Jason Draft's. He is the type to have seven hundred friends. Everybody he ever met in high school, work, college, games, bars. That person will . . . what?

Truly, what is she expecting to achieve here?

Snuffling happily at the front door is Barrel. How come he's loose?

Maybe the housekeeper has let Barrel out so that Miranda will be distracted while a drug delivery is made next door. Except that the Nevilles don't have water access or dock rights, and their cliff is even steeper and rockier than hers. Maybe the delivery is made to our dock, thinks Miranda. Maybe the drug dealer crashes through the bushes like any other young man and drops the package at the Nevilles' front door, like FedEx.

Having recently cleaned the living room, she doesn't want Barrel inside. The iPad in hand, she slips out of the house. It is hideously hot on the front porch. There is not even a ceiling fan to riffle the heavy air. Barrel himself is so hot it's like standing next to a fireplace. She lacks the energy to trudge all the way over to his run and put him back.

But it doesn't matter.

Down the driveway comes a Crown Vic. The bright-orange rectangle of the iPad in her hand is highly visible. Everything she does is too late and wrong.

She can't help it. She's crying again. She has a headache from all this crying. The detective from yesterday sits down with her. "How come you're in the front yard, Miranda? The view is in back."

"I was saying good-bye to the minister. And Jack was here to tell me he's going to a ball game. And Barrel is loose. He's always loose."

"May I have Lander's iPad, please?"

She hands him Lander's iPad. "I haven't even found out anything about Jason Draft yet."

He sits on the step and pats it and she sits too. "We'll look together." He enlarges one of the photos of Jason Draft.

"Jason Draft is real," the detective tells her. "We've got his high school record and his college record. We've been to his old neighborhood. His parents moved to Florida a few years ago, and we haven't found out where Jason lives now. He showed his ID as Jason Firenza when the barge incident happened. Maybe he purchased that online, easy enough to do. As Jason Draft, he has a huge friend list. We're working through it."

Miranda is dizzy with all the things the police have done in—what?—forty-eight hours, maybe. And what has she done? Nothing. She hasn't even managed to clean up an egg.

"So, Miranda, did you do all this stuff accusing Jason Firenza? The Facebook, the tweets, the Tumblr?"

"Um. Kind of."

"Somebody helped?"

"Um. Kind of. But the point is, I'm helping my sister."

"You're a good sister, Miranda. But here's the deal. Nothing, *nothing at all,* is good about drug dealers. No matter what level—running cartels in South America or delivering cocaine packages to the shoreline—drug dealers are dangerous. They are greedy. Quick to panic. Always on the edge of betraying or being betrayed."

She hates being lectured. She has already read all this stuff online.

"Listen to me, Miranda. Dealers are always armed. And here's the other thing. They're always high."

Miranda shrugs.

"Miranda, do you know what 'high' means? It doesn't mean happy and giddy and pleased with the world. It means everything is off. Your judgment, your timing, your emotions, your decency."

"Lander didn't know anything about that! Lander isn't that person! She doesn't know people like that!"

"She knows Jason. She was probably swept away by him. But not recently, Miranda. You're the one who took the photograph that shows how close they are." From his briefcase he takes Miranda's iPad, in Lander's mint-green case, and hands it to her. "Miranda, it's possible for you to go on posting, searching, asking. But I don't want you to. Your parents wouldn't want you to if they had any idea what's going on. Jason may be very handsome and he is definitely very glib, but under that pretty skin, he is very bad."

"But my *sister* isn't bad. I have to get her out of this."

"You have to stay away from this. The man you're trying to find doesn't want to be found. You let us do it. No drug dealer works alone. He has bosses and colleagues and runners and customers. You can't tell what you'll step into."

Miranda is stepping into nothing. It is the Internet. There are dozens, maybe hundreds, of responses on Lander's Facebook page. No one is going to think about Lander's little sister, whose existence and name they do not even know.

"I don't want you to be alone here," says the detective, and immediately she is not alone, because Henry and Hayden are racing over. "We had lunch!" screams Henry. "Let's walk Barrel again!"

"Does the other brother talk?" asks the detective softly.

"Hayden mainly listens. I don't think there's anything wrong with him. They just share life and Henry's share is speech."

The detective smiles at her. Miranda is good at making friends. Lander, not so much. Miranda's heart is pierced again with fear for Lander. Good people, like this detective, believe Lander is a killer.

The detective is reassured by the presence of little boys. He drives away, content in the thought that Miranda is not alone.

Her plan, if she can give it such a grandiose term, is to study Jason Draft's friend list. Read every post on Lander's Facebook page. Collate information. But the police are on that. They have squadrons of experts who can do everything faster and better than she can.

The boys wrestle each other and Barrel.

The heat thickens.

Miranda feels as if centuries pass. Summers are always slow, but this particular Sunday is lasting forever.

A van inches down the driveway. The logo of the Hartford television station is bright and gaudy on its side. A big professional camera pokes out the open passenger door.

"Get out!" screams Miranda. "Get out! Get out of here!"

The camera points at her. Probably the sister of the killer is pretty good copy too.

She wants to attack the van. Beat her fists on it. Kick it. But they will film her and the evening news will show proof that both Allerdon girls are violent.

Geoffrey appears. His towel is wrapped skirt-style around his waist. His bushy hair is wild, half wet, half dry. He walks slowly up to the van, squinting, as if the huge logo is difficult to read. He is not an authority figure. His hands dangle at his sides. They are huge hands. Football hands. His body, although large, does not yet match the size of the hands.

He stands by the open window like a big galoot. The towel falls to the ground, revealing green-and-black-striped swim trunks. With his huge football hand, Geoffrey grips the snout of the camera and wrenches it away.

"Hey!" shouts the crew.

Geoffrey swings the camera loosely in his huge fingers, as if he might drop it and say, *Oh, goodness. A smashed camera. What a shame.*

The crew is cursing now, telling Geoffrey he's a thief.

"Drive out," says Geoffrey in a bored-sounding voice. "I'll give it back to you when you're out in the road. The public road. Where you belong." He has his cell phone in his other hand. His fingers are so large Miranda can't imagine how he manages the keypad. Into the phone Geoffrey says, "The police just left the Allerdon property but we need them back. There are trespassers."

"We're going, we're going!" yells the van driver, reversing and making a tight circle. They want their camera more than they want to film Miranda.

Geoffrey walks ahead of the van, leading it up the drive, and they disappear beyond the trees. Miranda tries to see through the trees; see if the TV van is really leaving. All she can spot are glittering bits of glass high on the hill. Stu's half-hidden house. Is he watching?

She is filled with horror. The *world* is watching. The world is waiting with sick bated breath to see what else happens with Lander Allerdon and her family.

Geoffrey comes back.

The police come back.

Miranda wants to faint. Go, go, go, *go!* she thinks. Everybody, go.

At last everybody but Geoffrey and the little boys are gone.

"Are we still going to walk Barrel?" asks Henry hopefully.

Geoffrey sighs. "First, lock the house, Miranda."

He's handsome, actually. Miranda is amazed. How has she not noticed this? The big features are coming together in a big way: when all his body parts catch up to each other, Geoffrey is going to be a hunk. Miranda is embarrassed for not noticing before and even more embarrassed that she's noticing now. "I'm not sure where the key is," she admits.

"I'll wait while you find it," he says, like an older brother, complete with irritation.

"I know where it is!" shrieks Henry. He dashes inside, returns with a key and proudly locks the front door.

Geoffrey sighs again. "You can't just lock the front." He takes the key, goes in again, bolts the back two doors that open onto the screened porch, walks out the front, key-locks that door and hands Miranda the key.

"Thank you," she whispers. "Thank you for everything, Geoffrey."

But she feels ill. The cottage truly does lie open. Little children know where the keys are, neighbors pee in their toilet, TV stations know where the drive is.

She has a sense of a thousand mistakes that nobody in the Allerdon family even knew were mistakes. All their bad choices are piling up, making mountains and cliffs, and they're going to fall off that cliff, and it will be their own fault.

The boys share Barrel's leash and tumble after the dog. They could be exploring a jungle, they are so excited. What a day! TV vans, police cars!

Miranda trudges after them. Geoffrey seems to be waiting for something but she is too tired to look back at him.

I have to solve *something,* she thinks. Although a person who doesn't even have the key to her own cottage probably won't find the key to an unsolved murder.

She puzzles about the package of cocaine left in the boat. She doesn't know anybody who does drugs or would ever deal them. But statistically, that cannot be true. She must know plenty of them, and is too dense to see, or they are too clever to be seen.

Why would Jason abandon the package? And how did he get safely away before the police came, while Lander didn't?

The boat in which Jason and Lander arrived at that little swamp has been towed by the Coast Guard, and—of course—somebody has videoed this and put it online, and everybody has seen the *Water Fever*. It's just a little skiff with a single storage compartment.

Maybe Jason couldn't risk Lander seeing the package. Didn't dare lean into the skiff, grab a plastic bag filled with white stuff and say, *Just getting my coke. Back in a minute. Stay put, Lanny.*

But if Lander could go along with a murder, she could surely go along with a package.

It's all so stupid.

Maybe that's what crime is. Things go wrong, everybody panics, they do stupid things, and Miranda can't look for a rational explanation because nothing was ever rational.

Hayden has to pee, so the walk ends after a few hundred yards and everybody goes into the Warren house, including Barrel. Mrs. Warren stops folding little jeans and T-shirts and offers a cold drink.

Miranda believes that Mrs. Warren meant to love domestic life; she meant to homeschool her children, take up quilting and make her own jam. But in fact, Mrs. Warren hates all this stuff.

Surely if the Warrens were drug runners, they would be rich, and they would hire somebody else to fold the laundry.

Mr. Warren thanks Miranda for bringing the boys home,

because now they are going to hike in the nature preserve. It isn't Miranda's impression that the Warrens like nature any more than they like housekeeping. She is touched that they love the boys enough to risk tick bites for them.

Or they're making a drug drop out in the woods.

Miranda heads home, with Barrel and without the boys. She doesn't know whether to laugh or cry at the way she suspects everybody in the entire neighborhood. She remembers at last that she meant to check everybody else's Facebook page too.

Silly.

The neighbors are just living their lives, making sandwiches, playing video games, watching the river, brushing their teeth. They're not drug traffickers. And if they are drug traffickers, there won't be a statement on their bios.

Her mother's ring tone sounds. Miranda gets her cell phone out of her pocket. She's calmer with that rectangle in her hand. She feels purposeful, as if just holding a cell phone is a solution. "Hi, Mom."

"We've seen her."

"Is she okay?" This is a stupid question. Miranda doesn't know why she asks it.

Lander can't possibly be okay.

"No. She looks awful. Sort of grimy and wasted."

"Oh, Mom! Did you get to hug?"

"No. No, she's—behind—well—they're sort of separate rooms. We weren't really in the same room. Glass. Little shelves, sort of."

Her brilliant, articulate mother cannot describe a partition. Her daughter is on the other side of a barrier. The criminal side.

"And what did she say?"

"She said she loves us."

Lander does not deny the charges.

Miranda stops walking. Leans on a tree trunk. It's an oak, and the striated bark is rough against her skin.

"We met again with the lawyer. The arraignment is scheduled for tomorrow afternoon. Monday. It'll be on Monday. Tomorrow."

"What happens at an arraignment?"

"Well, it turns out that the police arrest a person, but the prosecuting attorney brings the charges, and that is done in front of a judge. The person is formally advised of the charges against them and told what their constitutional rights are. It's a very short event. The person doesn't say anything except 'not guilty.'"

The person.

Miranda weeps for her parents. "Is that when they set bail?" she asks. "Can we afford bail on the money we're getting from Grandma?"

Her mother is openly crying now. "There might not be bail. They don't usually have bail for homicide charges. She has to stay there, in that jail, behind those bars. Without us."

The arraignment will be in a courtroom. There will be no partitions. Miranda is definitely going to this. She will sit directly behind Lander. She has seen this in many TV shows.

Maybe it was an accident, she thinks. Lander and Jason accidentally killed Derry, but they didn't know it was Derry, and Jason ran off and she stayed. Except that Lander wouldn't just stand there if somebody was hurt. She'd love to stanch a bleeding wound. She'd love to rip her T-shirt into bandages while calling 911.

"Your father and I are driving back to West Hartford to get us all good clothes for the arraignment."

How desperate her mother must be, pretending that how the family is dressed will favorably impress a judge in a homicide case.

"We'll stop by and get you, honey," says her mother.

Since the quickest route to West Hartford is on the other side of the river, picking up Miranda is an hour out of the way. "No. I'm fine here. I've been playing with Henry and Hayden and Barrel." As if she, too, is a seven-year-old on a happy summer day. As if she is not involved in Lander's nightmare. "I love you," she says helplessly.

And she does love them. The shocking fact of their disregard for the future, specifically Miranda's future, is easy to table. At least, for now.

She and Barrel stumble home. Coming down the driveway, seeing the cherry-red siding of the little cottage, the green shutters that sag, the torn screened door, she thinks, If Lander never comes home, we might as well sell the cottage. We'll *want* to sell it. It will be nothing but the place where everything went wrong.

9

The lawyer discusses the arraignment.

How Lander will face a judge on Monday afternoon.

How her parents are bringing clothing so that she will look her best.

How she will be transported.

How she is to address the judge. "Your Honor," not "sir" or "ma'am."

How she is to say absolutely nothing except "not guilty" when the time comes.

The lawyer's face swims in and out of view.

Lander whispers to this woman her parents have chosen, "But I don't know what happened. I was there, but I don't know. *What if I am guilty?*"

This is the question she screams silently at God. *Am I*

a killer? Don't let me be a killer. Don't let Derry be dead because of me!

Do I really think God will go back in time and change my actions? Change the results? she asks herself. Or am I facing real consequences for the first time in twenty-two years, and I want God to be responsible instead of me?

The lawyer, like the police, has no patience with Lander's self-indulgent whining. She leans into Lander's face. "Your response is *'Not guilty.'* Do you grasp this?"

With her free hand, Lander reaches for a tissue from the box on the table.

"Lander!" snaps the lawyer. "Toughen up. It's not going to get easier. Tears don't soften judges."

She is not expecting to soften anybody. The pitiful truth is that she, Lander, is soft.

She has always seen herself as a woman of courage. A woman who marches through any difficulty, shrugs off any burden. A woman who could practice medicine in the midst of some distant civil war, saving lives while bombs drop. Instead, she is a weakling who needs her own tissue box just to cope with the loss of her cell phone.

Seeing her parents earlier in the day was an ordeal.

Her father looked terrible. He was nicely dressed, which is always the case. He loves clothing. He has more clothing than any of them. He loves shirts with collars and heavy starch. He loves ties and bow ties, vests and bright socks. He loves shoes. But the body inside this fine clothing was hunched and awkward. He tried to smile, but it didn't work. His face twitched.

Her mother looked worse. Her clothing was all ajumble, as if she couldn't find the buttons, couldn't fasten the necklace, couldn't pull the brush through her hair. Her mother was confounded by the barrier between them and several times put her hands against the thick, soiled glass, as if hoping it was a mirage.

They didn't know how to question her.

They said, "We love you, sweetheart," which is what people say when there is no point in addressing the situation.

She loves them back. She loves them so much she cannot believe she has ever ignored them, disobeyed them or shrugged them off.

She could not comfort them. There was no solid truth to set down in front of them, a daughter's lovely gift of innocence. "I love you, too," she told them. "Thank you for coming. Give Rimmie a hug. Tell her she was right about everything."

"Right about everything?" echoed her father.

"Rimmie knew all along that Jason was bad company," she explained, aware that a court verdict might be that she, Lander, was the bad company.

She was relieved when they left. Being in a cell was better than facing her terrified parents.

STILL SUNDAY AFTERNOON

The cottage is exhaustingly hot. Miranda can't stand being shut in. She opens every window, exposes every screen, unlocks every door. Not one shiver of breeze enters. But at least she doesn't feel like a trapped animal.

Lander *is* a trapped animal.

Miranda feels like having ice cream, but after two days of eating nothing, perhaps she should have a little something prior to dessert. In the kitchen she spots Mrs. Crowder's casserole. It's been sitting out since yesterday, in the hottest room in the cottage, facing the hottest sun. She lifts the lid. It stinks. It's totally gone bad.

Now on top of everything else she has to get rid of eight or ten helpings of something Mrs. Crowder slaved over.

The cottage doesn't have a garbage disposal.

She can't feed it to Barrel.

They don't even have garbage pickup. It's easier to lug a plastic bag back to West Hartford than to haul big trash cans up to the road, where they are out of sight, and the Allerdons forget them, and wind blows them into the middle of the road.

Her mother phones again. "I need your advice. What clothes should I choose? I don't know what to wear. I don't know what she should wear. I don't know what you should wear."

"What did Lander say to get for her?"

"She just shook her head."

"Meaning she doesn't care?" Caring is the hallmark of Lander's existence. She cares about grades, achievement, schools, success and all the accessories needed to display them.

"Oh, honey, I think she's in shock. She's hardly saying a word."

They're all in shock. But at least Miranda is at the cottage, not in a cage.

Lander seldom wears a dress or a skirt. So although those would be formal, and perhaps formal is good in front of a judge, Lander's best outfits are suits. "How about that pale-gray silk suit?" says Miranda. "The pants are solid and the jacket has tiny white dots and the cut is businesslike. And she could wear her white silk tee. Maybe a scarf. Not too much color in the scarf maybe. And those black strappy sandals? Because in heels she's five eleven. Maybe she'd look threatening? We want her to look, you know, sweet and girlish."

"I'm standing in front of her closet now. Yes, I see the suit. Good choice. And maybe the scarf that's white with turquoise streaks? She likes turquoise." Her mother's voice is brighter. Way easier to think about color than arraignments.

"Okay, then," says Miranda. "You've got the clothes. Bring her shampoo and conditioner and makeup. I think they let a person get ready. Now let's decide what you're going to wear. How about that navy dress with the silver chain belt? The one that's so flattering because of the way the skirt hangs. It would be perfect for you."

This may be the most ridiculous statement Miranda has ever made. On Monday, nothing is going to be perfect for her mother.

But they settle the clothing issue.

"I'll iron everything," says her mother, eager for a chore at which she can succeed. "I'll have it all on hangers." As if wrinkles matter. "We'll set off in about an hour, so we'll be at the cottage by nine. Lock the doors, honey. And the windows. I know you'll be hot and it will be awful. But . . ."

It's too late to lock up. There's no point in locking up. You can't lock out bad things. Look at Lander. She fell among bad people and fell into bad things and locks had nothing to do with it.

Miranda imagines the locks that now surround her sister.

Her mother presents another plan. "Maybe Daddy and I should just come and get you and we'll drive back here and sleep in the air conditioning. Yes. That's better. We need to be fresh and rested for tomorrow. We'll see you soon."

Normally Miranda never wants to be in West Hartford if she can be in the cottage, but it is so hot and she feels so awful. Is it hunger or despair? The prospect of her parents' arrival and an air-conditioned house ought to cheer her up, but it doesn't. Maybe she's past cheering up.

With a dish towel, Miranda wipes sweat off her face, considers again what to eat and again is confronted with Mrs. Crowder's rotting casserole.

The Crowders have an excellent position for drug dealing. Their house is virtually invisible, the way they've let the trees grow. A car can just slink up their driveway and disappear. Of course the same thing is true of Miranda's cottage. And the Warrens'.

I'll check out the Crowders on Facebook next, she decides.

It's energizing to have a plan, even a dumb one. She carries the heavy dish through the screened porch, down the steps, onto the grass and over to the cliff stairs. She unbolts the gate and carefully descends. If she spills now, she will also have to clean up the dock. Kneeling on the dock, she sets the lid down and lowers the casserole into the water, swishing it around. It'll be fine for fish, who don't seem to mind rotten anything.

She has a sudden insight into the delivery of all this food.

The reason their neighbors bring casseroles and gifts when her parents are not home is not that they dread speaking to her parents. The neighbors are sparing her parents. Giving the food to Miranda says *We're here for you* but does not force her parents to come face to face with pity.

Miranda loves her whole neighborhood all over again. She is free of suspicion. It is light and airy to feel this good.

She runs back up the cliff stairs. Everyone should have a skill and one of Miranda's skills is that she never grabs the handrail rope.

In the kitchen, she fills the empty casserole with soap and hot water and scrubs the pot and lid with a wire sponge. She heads out the front door to return them to Mrs. Crowder. She won't exactly lie about the fate of the food, but she won't tell the truth either. She'll say, *It was so kind! My parents are so glad you thought of us. How was your last trip? Was it Australia? Where are you going next?*

And then the dish will be off her hands, along with the guilt of feeding its contents to the fish.

She walks up the driveway to the little country road. To her right is the doctors' house, and farther down, she can see Geoffrey's house, and then Jack's.

She hasn't checked their Facebook pages either, but she doesn't care anymore. Parents who make cinnamon cookies, send fruit baskets and bake casseroles are not dealers. Boys who save you from TV crews, help you with online searches or put away the clean dishes for you are not enemies.

She crosses the street.

From their tree house, Henry and Hayden shriek, "Where are you going? Wait up! We want to come!"

Really, there are times when Miranda can't stand it. In West Hartford, she could circle the block ten times and nobody would notice. At the cottage she can't burp without witnesses.

But it is reassuring. Nobody here is doing anything clandestine or illegal. Henry and Hayden would know.

The boys race headlong, stumbling in their desperation to catch up. It doesn't seem to Miranda there has been enough time for the Warrens to trek down nature trails and already be home. Perhaps that is just Mr. Warren's excuse to get the murderer's sister away from his sons. Perhaps Mr. Warren is actually designing websites to transport illicit drugs all over the country.

Or perhaps I should get some sleep, Miranda thinks. At least have a sandwich.

The heat presses down again.

The light, airy relief of loving her neighbors is extinguished.

While she is amusing herself with fantasies, Lander is in jail. The arraignment is tomorrow. And what has Miranda accomplished? Zip.

She is too tired to deliver the silly casserole. Maybe she will just slip up to the side door, set it down and leave. But that is rude. That works only if she has a thank-you note to tuck into the dish.

The boys dance on their side of the street, begging her to come back and get them. They are not allowed to cross by themselves.

"No!" she yells. "Stay home!"

The Crowder driveway doubles in an S to diminish the steepness of the site. She drags herself up. The heat from the black asphalt is crazy. Her shoes may melt. The three-car carport is full, which is good. Everybody is here. It's been ages since she's seen Mrs. Crowder, proof that cars can come and go and, even here, nobody sees a thing.

The front door is many sweaty paces away. Miranda cuts through the carport to the side door. It is a glass storm door, with a panel that can be raised or lowered, so there's a screen if you want a breeze, or glass if you want air conditioning. It is currently open for a breeze, which is insane. The Crowders have central air. Anybody with air conditioning should be using it.

The doorbell is a small round button set in a small silver rectangle. Miranda balances the casserole against her left hip and raises her right hand to press the doorbell with her index finger.

What lies on the other side of the door is unlike anything she has ever seen. She cannot at first decide what it is. Indecision lasts a millisecond, and then she is throwing the casserole aside and racing down the drive. The heavy dish crashes against one of the parked cars.

She doesn't care about noise or damage. She has to get away from it. She has to get home.

The driveway tips down like a ski jump. She is afraid of tripping; afraid of falling. She tries to keep her balance and still run faster than she has ever run in her life. She gets her cell phone out. Do her fingers really know everything by memory? Can she hit 911 without looking, without slowing down?

Behind her a door bangs. The bang is too loud to be the flimsy side door. But no one could get out that door now anyway. Somebody is coming out the front door. Feet whack the pavement behind her.

Miranda screams.

The scream is unplanned. Unwanted. And she can't stop. Screams rip out of her chest, so violently they seem to tear her throat.

This is panic, she thinks. Did Lander panic? Did she shoot Derry Romaine by accident and then she panicked?

Miranda nears the street. She glances left and right. Traffic would be good; she'd love traffic; but there isn't any. What comes between her and the safety of home is a pair of happy yelling little boys.

"What are we doing? What's the game?" yells Henry, jumping up and down. "Why are you screaming?"

"Go home!" She brushes at them as if they are fallen leaves and she can rake them away. "Run home! Get out of here!"

They don't move. Home is boring. Miranda is exciting. They want to scream and run down hills, too.

The pounding feet behind her catch up.

She whirls in terror.

But it is only Stu.

"Oh, Stu!" she gasps. "Oh, Stu, did you see it? Oh, thank goodness you're here. And you're safe! Thank goodness you're safe!"

Her trembling fingers fail to find 911. Stu takes the phone out of her hand. "I'll do it," he says. He turns to Henry and Hayden. "You boys run on home now. It's suppertime."

How can he be so calm? A dead body lies on his kitchen floor. Blood has spattered every appliance.

Stu does not call 911. He drops her phone into his own jeans pocket. Miranda stares at the pocket; at the thick denim and the double row of stitching. *Stu is not calling the police.*

"We ate a long time ago," says Henry, not leaving.

In Stu's other hand, held close to his thigh, where the little boys cannot see it, is a knife. It is not a kitchen knife. Its peculiar blade is sharp on both sides. She is not sure what such a knife is meant for.

The blade is bloody.

She remembers the expert. *Drug dealing is a young man's game.* And here stands the only young man in the neighborhood. A man the same age as Jason Draft and Derry Romaine. A man who came three times to Miranda's house to ask how Lander is doing. A man excited by the possibility of Lander's suffering.

Stu's eyes are wide with shock. He is shaking.

Well, of course he is. There is a dead body in his house and Stu is probably holding the knife that sliced the body to pieces.

Is Stu the one who did it? Or is he terrified of the person who did?

Stu's eyes flicker madly, and again she is reminded of squirrels that bite their way through screens.

Nothing is good about drug dealers. They are greedy. Quick to panic.

Miranda's own panic drops away.

She could grab the boys' hands, and race them across the grass, through the trees and into their house.

But what will Stu do if three people turn their backs and run?

If it were not for the blood and the knife, she would not be considering him as a murderer. She's still not sure. But she cannot let him take the boys hostage. Or worse. She says firmly, "Henry. Hayden. Home. Now."

The boys' little shoulders sag. They walk away slowly, knowing that the good stuff is here and boring stuff awaits them at home. They'll have to take a bath. And go to bed. But over at Miranda's, people are screaming and running down hills and chasing each other!

Henry taunts his brother. "Hay-den is a slowpoke."

"Am not!" shrieks Hayden.

It is amazing how much racket two little boys running on grass can make. They pass through the backyards of the two neighbors who are rarely here. She cannot see them now but she knows they are pummeling each other, giggling, grabbing each other's shirts, trying to win the race.

"Get in the cottage," whispers Stu. His hand is shaking so badly that the knife could be a spoon, stirring cake batter.

Drug dealers, lectured the detective, *are always armed. And here's the other thing. They're always high.*

Miranda Allerdon is standing with a murderer who is panicked, armed and high.

He's looking back and forth, up and down. She has the sense that he cannot believe what is happening. That he's hoping to see some way out. But there's only grass and trees and a dead body in the kitchen.

She forgets that Stu has another hand and it is not holding anything. Stu's free hand flashes forward. He threads his fingers through a hank of her hair. Miranda's hair is not elegant, swinging and shiny like Lander's. Loose, Miranda's hair is a pyramid of curly frizzy brown. Stu twists the hair.

A murderer now controls Miranda the way she controls Barrel on his leash.

10

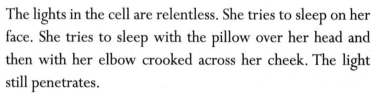

The lights in the cell are relentless. She tries to sleep on her face. She tries to sleep with the pillow over her head and then with her elbow crooked across her cheek. The light still penetrates.

In real life, she would never be in bed this early. But there is absolutely nothing to do here. And because this *is* her real life—she really is here; there really are bars—sleep is the only escape.

"Can we turn off some of the lights?" she begs. "Or dim them?"

"No. Prisoners like you are under observation. You might try suicide."

Suicide?

Her? Lander?

She has never thought of taking her life. In fact, novels assigned in middle school and high school often dwell on adolescent suicide. She is irked by these plots, and skips those chapters. Life is wonderful, the future will be better and who could possibly want to exit early?

But the word lingers.

"Suicide."

If she peeks into the future outlined by the bars and the metal bed shelf, she can see why a person might consider it.

She slams her mind shut against the word. She will live in the minute.

This bright white glaring minute reveals nothing of how she came to be here and whether she is guilty. It reveals only the perfidy of Jason. She can think of no reason for him to ruin her. She is beginning to conclude that he did it for fun.

It's in the news sometimes—where young men in gangs kill people for fun. *Just wanted to see what it was like,* they say, smirking.

Is Jason out there somewhere, smirking?

Lander buries her face in the thin pillow and sobs.

SUNDAY EVENING

Miranda imagines Stu carrying his kayak down from his house to her little dock. Inflating it. Paddling slowly and alone down the river to meet some other boat, and take some delivery. Not marijuana, which comes in bales and would be too large and smell too strong. But drugs that take little space. Heroin. Cocaine. Perhaps that's what the cup holder is for.

She has thought all along that the water has something to do with it; that somehow delivery and sale and money all glide along the river.

But it doesn't start in front of our house, she thinks. It starts in front of Stu's house. I was going in the right direction. But I would never have gotten there. I would never really have thought that somebody I know would do this.

"Go inside," Stu says very softly, as if the world is listening.

But the world is not listening and it is not looking. When they step through the thick band of shrubs and trees that wrap the Allerdon yard, they are alone.

Stu's teeth are chattering. She has never heard anybody's teeth click like that. The hand holding her hair has a tremor so intense that her scalp rattles. Stu is more terrified than she is.

Because he can picture the body in his kitchen?

Because he's in shock that he actually used a knife on a man's flesh?

Because his neighbor Miranda knows? And can tell?

What did happen at the top of that S-curved driveway? The chances are that Stu did not plan to murder anybody in his kitchen. The chances are that some rage swept over Stu, or perhaps over the victim. A kitchen is full of weapons, and Stu got there first.

With the knife that is now lightly poking her in the back.

How hard will he push that knife into her skin? How much damage will it do? Will he use that knife on her as many times as he used it on Jason?

Because that's who it is.

Jason.

Drug dealers are always on the edge of betraying or being betrayed.

Did Jason betray Stu? Did Stu betray Jason?

But why don't these people just yell at each other and

then grill a hamburger? Why do they kill each other? How can it matter that much?

Far away, a door slams. Henry and Hayden are inside their house. They know how to call 911. They could save her. But they think Miranda and Stu are playing games.

Stu is panting. He pants like Barrel, mouth open, trying to cool himself off.

Stu is in a situation he cannot want. There are too many bodies now. He can't add another one and get away with it. She has to convince him of that. But what can she offer? Silence? He knows perfectly well she'll call the police the first chance she gets.

She drags her feet. The knife penetrates her shirt. Enters her flesh. She tries to get away but he is holding her hair. She can only arch her spine, as if an inch will help.

Perhaps for Stu and Jason, it is all a game. A crazy profitable fun game, sneaking around with kayaks and stolen boats, grinning at each other, having a beautiful girl on your arm. But it's not a game now that Stu has killed Jason. It will not end like a game. Nobody will fold up the board, put away the cards or collect the dice.

In front of her, the sun is sinking. The western sky is magnificent. It is a photograph night, with colors so wild and impossible it could be the beginning or the end of the world.

Stu's grip on her hair forces her head backward, exposing her throat. It occurs to Miranda that Lander lucked out. She's safe behind bars.

"In!" says Stu again. His whole body is having tremors; probably his whole brain.

Once they are both inside, he lets go of her hair.

She turns. For a moment they just stare at each other. She cannot think how to escape and he cannot think what to do with her. Anger is overtaking Stu's fear. Miranda is ruining everything.

He jabs the knife forward, not close enough to touch her, but she leaps out of range, and he is weirdly entertained. They cross the living room like this.

Jab!

Jump!

Jab!

If I had gone to Stu's Facebook page instead of the Warrens', I might have found Jason among his friends, she thinks. Or if I had gone to Jason's page—Jason Draft's, that is—I might have found Stu. I might have figured this out. The police are working on those friend lists. But do they even know who Stu is? Will they recognize his picture? Probably. But not in the next two minutes, which is when I need them.

"Get on the porch," he orders.

She steps outside. The porch bakes like an oven. There is not a whisper of breeze.

Her only hope is reminding him that he likes her; he likes the whole family; he probably still has his crush on Lander. "Stu, what's happening?" she whispers.

"What's *happening?*" Stu shouts. Rage seems to come out of his pores as well as his mouth. "Jason was supposed to drown Derry. He was supposed to take Derry north to the marshes around the old nuclear power plant. Hundreds of acres. Nobody lives there, nobody goes there. But Jason saw that barge coming and decided to improvise. He loved the idea that all those witnesses would watch a murder and not even know. But it didn't work. Derry survived!"

And now, horribly, Stu is crying. Tears run down his face. Mucus comes out his nose. Is he full of regret or full of his drug of choice?

Miranda doesn't scream. There is no one to hear. The doctors Neville are never around Sunday evenings; they've already returned to Hartford. The two houses between her and the Warrens are not occupied this weekend. Henry and Hayden, the neighborhood spies, are safely inside and probably arguing about bedtime.

Last Saturday, when she and Stu were chatting next to Barrel's run, Stu was shocked to hear that the water skier survived the barge. Was he shocked, she wonders now, because he planned that murder? "Why kill Derry?" she asks.

"I make a ton of money, Rimmie," says Stu. He laughs a little, as if acknowledging that money will not offset the situation he is in now. "I do college campuses. I have a stable of guys like Derry. He was keeping money that wasn't his."

Miranda means to let him babble. Words will ease him. She will think of a compromise. But she forgets her plan.

"Okay," she says irritably, having earned the right to be irritable; the creep is jabbing a knife at her. "But what does my sister have to do with it?"

"Lanny wouldn't go out with me again. She had better things to do with her time. She even said that, right to my face! 'My time is precious,' she said." Stu mimics a high-pitched nasty little female voice. Miranda cannot imagine Lander speaking like that. Although she would certainly say it. For Lander, it is simply a fact; her time is precious.

"I say to Lander—'What? Too precious to waste on me?'"

Stu has backed her halfway across the porch and now Miranda's hand is close to the knob of the kitchen door. If she rips it open fast enough, and leaps inside and throws the bolt, she can race to the other inside door and bolt that, and then bolt the front, and then use the landline to call the police!

"Do you know what your sister did?" screams Stu. "She shrugged! She walked off. She drove away. I asked her out again. I have lots of money. We can do anything. She didn't even look up."

Lander has treated her younger sister like this. Miranda knows how much it hurts. Lander does not even bother to raise or harden her voice when dismissing somebody. Lander really and truly forgets that person immediately.

"And then," says Stu, brushing away his tears, "Lander went out with Jason. My runner. He's nobody. And she fell in love with him." Stu is weeping for Lander. Not for the

216

body on his kitchen floor. But for the girl who didn't love him back.

"Lander wouldn't even have a second cup of coffee with me!" cries Stu. "But for Jason she turned into a puppy wagging her tail, hoping Jason would pat her little head."

Miranda's hand flashes out to the kitchen doorknob.

This time when Stu slashes he is not teasing. She is so shocked to see her flesh laid open that she doesn't cry out. She wraps the bleeding hand in the cloth of her T-shirt. She is afraid to think about the damage. Will her hand still work? It's her right hand. She's right-handed. Has he cut through her tendons?

"Don't do that!" screams Stu. "Don't get in my way! You shouldn't have gotten in my way! Too many people are getting in my way!"

Is Stu about to finish her off the way he finished Jason? Miranda wants Stu to talk, not slash. "Derry got in the way?"

Stu's rage abates. His tears dry. He's sufficiently aware to wipe his nose on the bottom of his T-shirt.

They are both panting with exhaustion.

"Derry was thrilled when I got him out of that hospital," says Stu. He looks sad and confused. He frowns a little, as if remembering a distant decade. "See, if they identify or fingerprint Derry, it's not good, because he's got warrants out under his real name. Prison was going to be his next stop. When I tiptoed in with street clothes, he thought we were buddies." Stu looks puzzled. Maybe he too thought they were buddies. "Derry thought when I drove down a deserted driveway and we parked the car and I helped him down a footpath into the marsh that I had some great boat for him to escape in." Stu's teeth are chattering again. "No, but I had a nice bullet."

Stu killed Derry.

Lander had nothing to do with it.

This is wonderful to know but useless. The information doesn't count unless the police have it. Miranda cannot phone or text them. She cannot quickly write a note for them to find.

Her back is against the last door: the door that opens to the steps, the grass, the cliff and the river. Will he push her over the edge? Drown her? There are two big old wooden chairs on the grass, the painted kind that look like comfy recliners, but without piles of puffy cushions they're unsittable. She can get a chair between herself and Stu. And then what? Run in little tiny circles around the chair until her parents get here?

And how will her parents know to be afraid of Stu Crowder?

What if Stu holds them all hostage?

"But, Stu, how did you make it look as if Lander did it?"

"I had to talk Jason into it. But he's a druggie, you know. It's easy to corner a druggie. Once Derry was dead, I texted Jason that we were all set and he brought old Lander in on that little skiff they stole. She was all giggly and eager to please. She couldn't even stay for a whole evening with me, but for Jason she picked up a gun, when she thinks guns are for sickos, and she shot it because Jason told her to, and beamed at him and hoped for her reward. She was a dog wanting a treat."

Stu is nodding weirdly. The nod includes his entire upper body. The nod includes the knife hand. He is stuck in bobbing motion. He points the shivering knife toward the last door. She has to turn her back on him and she doesn't want to turn her back and she's slow and not thinking, and again he threads the fingers of his free hand through her hair. Her plan to run is ridiculous.

"So then," Stu says, "Jason walked away. Old Lander just stood there like a good puppy. I'd already called in a tip to the state police. We dropped our disposable phones in the water and the two of us left in another boat. Easy peasy."

The cliff stairs are not visible from a single house on the river. If Stu shoves her off the cliff, she won't be able to swim out and save herself. There is a rock shelf, which is why the fishing is good. She will go neck-first into the rocks.

"We had to get rid of Derry anyway," says Stu, "so I figured, why not give old Lander something to do with that precious time of hers? She's so proud of being Little Miss Perfect. I'll make her Little Miss Killer. And all that precious time? It'll be hard time now. That's precious. None of her friends have that."

Miranda remembers a sermon. *Much sin,* said the minister, *stems from the love of money and the pain of love.*

I will never know love or the pain of love, thinks Miranda. I will be dead.

Stu twirls her by the hair until he can look down into

her eyes. He is in pain. Not as much pain as Miranda, with him yanking her hair off her scalp. But the terrible things he's done lie just behind his eyes, and he can't look away from what he's done.

"You're just like her, Rimmie." His voice breaks like a little boy's. "I offered to help you with your online search and you shut the door in my face. Remember that? Remember how you didn't have time for me either? So I'll give you even more precious time than I'm giving your sister. I'll give you eternity."

She'll be fish food, like the casserole. Who really made that casserole? Is Mrs. Crowder actually living in that house with that blood-spattered kitchen? Or are the parents in Australia? Did *Stu* make the casserole? She imagines him draining noodles while dreaming of Lander in prison.

"We're going to use my original plan, Rimmie. We're going to take your Zodiac. I've got your cell phone. Isn't that handy? In a little while, your parents will get a text from you. It will say *I'm feeling so sad, I wish I were dead.* And you will be! Fun, huh?"

Stu is weeping again. Nothing is fun about this, not for him and not for her.

She actually pities him. He has made bad friends, bad judgments, bad moves, and no matter what he does now, he's going to get caught. The blood in his kitchen can never be removed. Stu will get no do-over. He's twenty-three and he's destroyed himself along with Derry and Jason, and he knows it.

220

But he's going down trying, and that means Miranda too will die.

What will an autopsy decide about the slash on her hand? The pinpricks in her back? What about Henry and Hayden, who know that Stu is the last person to be seen with Miranda? But Stu is way beyond caring about the holes in his plan.

He spins her by the hair until she is facing the bluff again, and again the knife is poking a tiny hole in her back.

Because of the long steep drop, she cannot see the river's edge or the dock. What she does see is the Zodiac slowly drifting downstream. Whoever tied it up last didn't do much of a job. She has a burst of hope. She will tear down the stairs, throw herself in the water, swim like a madwoman, catch the Zodiac and get away from Stu.

But he is bigger and will swim faster. Or he'll take the kayak Geoffrey so thoughtfully returned to the dock, and then Stu will catch both Miranda and the Zodiac.

Miranda has raced down these steps thousands of times. They are steep and tricky. But Stu has also used these steps a thousand times. She won't have much advantage.

"I can't balance with you ripping my hair out," she says irritably.

His fingers loosen. Not a lot, but enough. Miranda launches so hard she misses the top two steps and slides painfully down two more, the rough wood edges scraping open the backs of her bare legs. She grabs the sagging rope line, catches herself and stumbles down another step, way too slowly for escape.

Standing on the little dock below is Geoffrey, his fishing gear a mess all around him. He is holding up his arms. "Jump!" he yells. *"Jump!"*

She's too far up to jump.

Stu lets out a roar like a motorcycle. He hits the top step so hard it seems to splinter.

She hurtles down.

But Stu is taking the steps two at a time. He will be upon her in another second.

Miranda jumps.

It's a long way.

Geoffrey can't quite catch her, but he blocks her fall and manages to hurl both their bodies sideways into the river. They barely clear the dock. By the time they surface and rub the water out of their eyes, Stu has landed on the dock. Miranda and Geoffrey are within knife reach.

Stu falls to his knees and slashes. But Geoffrey's big lumpy body is strong. In two great strokes he moves himself and Miranda beyond Stu's reach.

"Stu," says Geoffrey calmly, "you've got time to get back to your house and get a car." Geoffrey takes another stroke back into the river.

Stu looks up the stairs. He looks over at the Allerdons' kayak.

"He'll put the kayak in the water!" Miranda cries.

"Doesn't matter. After I untied the Zodiac, I threw the

kayak paddle away. See it floating downstream? But does Stu have a gun, Rimmie? Because that would be lousy." Geoffrey is doing a one-armed backstroke, his other arm keeping Miranda afloat. They are quite a few yards away from the dock now.

"No. Just the knife. Geoffrey, Stu killed people!"

"I heard it all. He forgot the porch is open. Just let your legs hang there, Rimmie," says Geoffrey. "I'll do the swimming."

She's bleeding from the cut on her hand, but she isn't bleeding much and there are no sharks in the Connecticut River to smell the blood. Unless she counts Stu.

The air is so hot. The shock of the cool water gives her the shakes. She can't splint her cut hand and still hold on to Geoffrey. "I've got you," he says. "Just hang there."

Stu kicks off his shoes. He's going to swim after them. Or after the Zodiac.

Even bleeding from the wounds Stu gave her, Miranda cannot believe that there *is* a drug dealer on her sweet street. Her beloved river *is* a conduit for drugs. There *is* an industry in which people kill each other over powdered stuff.

"Geoffrey, Stu killed Jason. Jason was sort of all over the kitchen floor, all blood and smear, and I was just returning the casserole and I thought Mrs. Crowder was home because all three cars were there, but——"

Mrs. Warren appears at the top of the bluff.

Henry and Hayden will be at her side! Stu will have someone to hurt after all. He'll run back and attack them!

"No!" screams Miranda. "Go home! He's a murderer! He's got a knife!"

But it is not Henry or Hayden who appears next to Mrs. Warren. It's Mr. Warren and he has a rifle.

Stu looks up at the rifle and downriver at the drifting Zodiac. He is trapped. But he may not care about the rifle. He may race back up the steps, assuming Mr. Warren will not have the guts to shoot him; that he can still get away.

Miranda whispers in Geoffrey's ear, "It's Henry's toy rifle."

"Gotta love this neighborhood," says Geoffrey. She's shivering so hard that he needs both arms to keep her afloat, so he stops swimming and just treads water.

The river carries them down in front of the Neville property, whose rocky bluff does not allow river access. It will be half a mile downstream before there's another dock.

Stu is swearing, each word broken by a gurgling sob. He climbs back up the steps. He grips his knife. Mrs. Warren is angling a wooden lawn chair to the top of the stairs, clearly planning to topple it down on Stu.

Miranda closes her eyes. She has enough terrible images in her brain.

"She missed him," says Geoffrey regretfully.

Stu knows now that Mr. and Mrs. Warren are not going to shoot him, or they'd have done it. Will this encourage him? Will he now use the knife on them?

The big old trees and the thick pricker bushes that grow out of the Nevilles' cliff block Miranda's view.

The sun vanishes. The golden shimmer on the river is gone. The cold water is awful. She cannot see the remaining houses in the neighborhood, because of the bluff, but now they are passing Geoffrey's, and soon will pass Jack's. Then comes a freshwater tidal marsh owned by the Nature Society. Finally they will reach a house that's not part of their neighborhood; in fact, not on their road.

Geoffrey says, "Could you relax already? I swim this distance all the time."

She has just escaped a murderer, the murderer is advancing on Mr. and Mrs. Warren and Geoffrey wants her to relax?

In the distance, she hears a siren.

Sound carries on the water. The siren could be anywhere, on either side of the river. It could be a traffic stop. It could be rescue.

On a Sunday night, there is not a lot of boat traffic. People are exhausted from a day in the sun. They have gone home, thinking of dinner and a good movie. But Jet Skiers never tire.

In the awful split of hot air and cold water, of warm Geoffrey and evil Stu, a pair of Jet Skis appear. They zoom over. Is it the same set that rescued Derry? She doesn't know.

"You guys okay?" they ask. Because it is possible that a young couple would want to swim a few miles in each other's arms.

"No," says Geoffrey. "We aren't. Take her first. She's hurt."

"Do you have your cell phones?" Miranda begs the men. "Call nine-one-one."

"Hey," says Geoffrey. "You think I'm some kind of slouch? I called when I heard the very first word out of crazy Stu."

"Where's your phone, then?"

"Safe and dry in the Zodiac. You really do think I'm a slouch."

She is mounted on a Jet Ski now, holding the waist of a stranger.

The sirens are louder.

She folds like an old towel against the Jet Skier's back, and weeps.

Please let them get here in time to save Mr. and Mrs. Warren. Please don't let my parents drive in just as Stu needs a vehicle.

Instead of heading downstream for the dock, their rescuers move out into the middle of the river to see what's going on. "I can see lights whirling on police cars," says Miranda's savior. "The cops are driving right down to the river. I guess they're in somebody's yard."

Mine, thinks Miranda. They're here. They'll save the Warrens. They'll keep my parents safe.

Whatever Stu may claim later, he has confessed what really took place on Friday; who really committed the two murders. Geoffrey heard every word. Geoffrey will testify. Lander will go free.

Miranda knows the pain Stu's parents will face: the agony of a child gone bad.

Deep in her heart, Miranda did fear that Lander might have gone bad. She erases that thought from the screen of her mind. No one will ever know that she was not sure of her sister's innocence.

They accelerate downstream, arriving at the big beautiful dock whose owner does not have or even want a boat. It is a dock for sitting on. And there is the neighbor, sitting.

In a moment Miranda is wrapped in a cotton blanket. The neighbor whips out a first aid kit and bandages Miranda's hand. The Jet Skiers rescue the kayak paddle. Towing the Zodiac, they head back to Miranda's to watch the action.

The tight bandage eases the hurt in her hand.

Geoffrey helps Miranda into the front seat of the neighbor's car before he gets in back. It's a two-mile drive to connect with the lane on which Geoffrey and Miranda live, and when they finally arrive, the place is solid with police cars and whirling lights.

My neighborhood, she thinks, unable to take it in. A murderer lives across the street from *me*.

Geoffrey and the neighbor won't let Miranda get out of the car until they're sure Stu has been caught. "He got up the cliff steps okay," says a constable. "He just ran past Mr. and Mrs. Warren. Maybe he was scared of them or just didn't care about them. Anyway, he ran straight for the road. But he didn't cross the road. He didn't even try. When we got here, he was just standing on the side of the road crying."

Because he knew he would be caught anyway? Miranda wonders. Because he didn't want to look into his own kitchen or his own heart? Because he wishes Derry and Jason could still be alive and his life could still be a video game? Or did the high run out? And he was just a loser on the edge of nothing?

"He didn't put up a fight. He's cuffed and locked in a police car."

"What time is it?" Miranda whispers.

"Nine p.m.," says the constable.

It is exactly forty-eight hours since police arrived at the cottage to say that Lander was in jail. All this happened in one weekend.

The constables call an ambulance for Miranda.

"I don't want one! I want to stay here!"

Mrs. Warren appears. She and the helpful neighbor peel off Miranda's T-shirt to examine the punctures. "The punctures aren't deep," says Geoffrey. "I'm not sure you even need stitches. Well, maybe a few. And your hand—that needs stitches. And shots and stuff. No telling where that knife has been used before."

Miranda knows where it has been used before.

"How did you know to come over, let alone with a toy gun?" Miranda asks Mrs. Warren.

"Henry said Stu had a knife. He couldn't figure out what kind of game used a great big bloody knife. We couldn't think of one either, so we called the police. We couldn't wait for the police to get here, of course. We're so far out in the country. It could take ages. So we locked the boys in the house, grabbed the only gun we have, which is plastic and doesn't shoot, and came running. The officer told us that you found the body of Jason Firenza in Stu's kitchen. My poor girl. I'm so sorry you had to see that."

Clueless Mrs. Warren knows about Jason Firenza?

"Of course we knew," says Mrs. Warren impatiently.

"And you let the boys come over to my house anyway?"

"Miranda! We love you. The boys love you. Of course we let them. Any time we can take advantage of you, we do. You know that."

The constables retrieve Miranda's cell phone from Stu's pocket. They give it to her. There is a text message from her parents. We're almost there.

Mrs. Warren takes Miranda's phone and taps the dial-back button. Miranda hears her mother's voice: "Rimmie?"

"No, it's Wendy Warren here. Don't panic. Miranda is fine. I'm at the cottage with her. Stu Crowder is the murderer, not Lander. Miranda is the heroine of the day. She caught Stu. The police have Stu in custody. I don't think there will be an arraignment tomorrow. I think they will accept that Lander was a bystander."

It is a generous summary. Miranda does not feel like a heroine and in fact, she did not catch Stu. The police did. And it's Geoffrey who is the hero.

The ambulance is here.

"I don't want to go," she protests again.

"I'll go with you," says Geoffrey.

Mrs. Warren shakes her head. "No, Geoffrey, you stay here and tell the police everything Stu said. I'll go with

Miranda. Now buck up, Miranda. You protected my sons, you saved your sister, you're brave, brave, brave. You have the perfect name, too."

"I do?"

"Miranda. The name is Shakespeare's invention, you know. It means 'a woman to be admired.'"

At the hospital, she gets antibiotics, a tetanus shot and eleven stitches on the fat side of her hand. She hangs on to Mrs. Warren until her parents arrive in a police car with the siren going. Her parents are the most wonderful sight in the world.

They hold her and rock her. Then it is their turn to sob and they do it well, but Miranda is fine, partly because it's over, and partly because the doctors have given her a sedative.

Mr. Warren drives up to the hospital in the Warrens' massive van, with the boys in car seats in the middle row, thrilled to be up so late and part of the action. The three Allerdons squash into the back row of the van so that they can all go home together. The detectives follow in their own vehicles. They have a lot of questions for Miranda and Miranda has a lot of questions for them.

First she wants a shower. She has Stu's fingerprints in her hair.

"No," says her mother. "You have to keep the stitches dry. I'll sponge you off later."

The sedative makes her groggy. It will be crummy if she doesn't manage to stay awake for the rest of the evening. When they reach the cottage, Miranda is so worn out she can barely swing her feet out the van door. But once she is standing, she's okay.

The living room is full of neighbors and police.

Jack is here. Look what happens while he is wasting time on a ball game and a slow restaurant. He misses all the good stuff. Jack is grumpy.

Geoffrey, however, is pretty puffed up. He saved Miranda's life. Her father shakes Geoffrey's hand again and again, each time having forgotten the previous shake. Everybody slaps Geoffrey on the back. They are careful not to slap Miranda on the back.

Miranda starts her questions in the middle of nowhere. "Mr. and Mrs. Crowder aren't home after all, are they?"

"No," says a detective. "We don't know where they are. Most likely, Stu drove them to an airport months ago and has all three cars."

Mrs. Warren says, "We always thought Stu was weird. We joked about it. We'd say, *His parents aren't in Australia; Stu buried them in the basement.* It never occurred to me that Stu being weird had anything to do with Lander being arrested. It never occurred to me to tell the police that one of the neighbors is weird. I didn't think of Lander's nightmare as a neighborhood thing."

Miranda defends her precious neighborhood. "It wasn't a neighborhood thing. It was Stu and only Stu."

Everybody is starving. Miranda does not mention the casseroles in the refrigerator, although they are probably safe to eat. So improbable that the Allerdon family has ever had to think about murder and prison, let alone serial killers with casseroles.

Her father resorts to his favorite activity. He turns on the grill and tosses frozen hamburgers over the fire. It is a midnight cookout. The detectives are as hungry as everybody else. Henry and Hayden miss it because they fall asleep on the sofa.

"Why did Stu make a casserole?" asks Miranda.

"Maybe he needed an excuse to walk over and ask you about Lander. He may have hoped to hear that Lander was suffering. But he claims to love her, so maybe he was hoping to hear that there wasn't enough evidence, even though he's the one who set it up, and that Lander was on her way home."

The other detective says, "He may have made the casserole in order to pass himself off as the good neighbor. He might even think of himself as a good neighbor. Plus, he's a dramatic kind of guy. Needs props and occasions. Like the whole stupid attempt to drown Derry. Your normal drug dealer would just shoot the guy in the street and drive off."

Is there such a thing as a "normal" drug dealer? Miranda wonders.

She joins her father at the grill. He sets down his spatula to hug her (carefully) yet again.

I don't care that they never saved money for me, she thinks. I might care one day, when I have to go to college online instead of on campus, but right now, all I care about is that my family is safe.

"Daddy?" she says softly. She loves his size, his smell, his hug. "Will we still have to sell the cottage?"

He stares into the dark moonless night. Then he nods and shrugs at the same time, and Miranda sees written on his face all the debt, all the mistakes, all the overspending, all the bills yet to come. "Yes, baby. We will. There's no silver lining to this nightmare, Rimmie, but at least your mother and I recognize now that we can't be so careless about dollars."

How easily a person can make bad judgments.

Her parents made a lot of bad calls. Lander made the most of all.

Geoffrey made only good calls. Yet she hasn't really thanked Geoffrey, about whom she's had nothing but bad judgment. She has her actual life to thank him for. But even after all that's happened, and all that's gone down, Miranda is still awkward around a boy her own age. Even a boy in whose arms she has drifted downriver. Maybe especially a boy in whose arms she has rested.

Miranda can no longer make out her father's face. It must be getting dark very fast. But that doesn't seem right. It's been dark for a long time.

"She's asleep on her feet," says a voice. "Let's put her to bed."

It's delicious to be carried like a toddler.

To sleep as babies do, knowing that the world is safe.

11

Sunday night passes in an agony of sleeplessness, tears and regret. The whole word "arraignment" is a disaster. What will Monday be like?

Lander does not find courage during the long hours of fluorescent light and snoring prisoners, but she bottoms out. Whatever is coming, she can face it.

In the morning, they bring her to yet another interview room. They don't put cuffs on her. Perhaps they realize that she is beaten. How quickly I give up, thinks Lander. It isn't even seventy-two hours and I am whipped.

This isn't the same as the other interview rooms. It's a real room, with real windows, real furniture and a lot of people.

"So your sister, Miranda," says one of the detectives—

they all look alike to her, even the ones of different races; in her horror she cannot distinguish them—"is a heroine."

She is too exhausted to understand. "No, no! It's bad enough you're accusing me. Miranda would never do drugs. She would never touch heroin. Leave my sister out of this. She's a good person!"

The detective says, "Put an *e* on the end of the word 'heroin,' Lander. Your sister has saved you. She found out what really happened."

An *e* on the end of the word.

Heroine.

Miranda.

"She told us she'd rescue her sister, and she did. Along with some really great neighbors of yours."

They are actually smiling at her.

She is rescued? It's over? Miranda saved her?

Lander stares at the detective, wanting him to say that again.

"Stu Crowder killed Derry Romaine," says the detective.

"Stu?" How could Stu have anything to do with this?

"He deals," says the detective. "Mainly college campuses. Keeps records on his laptop. We're pretty happy with all we're going to learn from that laptop."

Boring Stu? All along he's been a dealer and a murderer? She almost argues with the police, it seems so improbable.

"One of his dealers was a man named Jason Draft. Jason Firenza to you. Stu also murdered Jason. That's why we couldn't find Jason. He was dead on the Crowders' kitchen floor."

Jason?

Wonderful, handsome, romantic Jason is dead on a kitchen floor?

She covers her face. It is wonderful to have free hands, but horrible to weep for the wasted life of Jason. Oh, Jason, I truly loved you, she thinks. No matter what you've done, I don't want you to be dead.

"The two of them set you up. It was both revenge and a game."

Stu and Jason were a team?

"Why wouldn't you talk to us about anything?" asks the detective. "The whole crime scene on the river was squirrelly, and the whole situation was cockeyed. If you had just talked to us, maybe we could have pieced things together earlier."

It's going to be my fault they were too dumb to figure it out? Lander glares at them, and anger rescues her a little bit. "I didn't know what happened!" she snaps. "I was the only one who shot that gun. And I'm *still* the only one who shot the gun! What if I really had killed somebody? I had to think it through. I couldn't say anything until I *knew*."

"Stu killed Derry before you got there. He wiped the gun and left it there for Jason to give you."

So when they arrived at that swampy little peninsula, Jason already knew that Derry was lying there dead. The target practice was a charade he had rehearsed. All his smiles and compliments were a game.

Miranda can think of nothing she has done to Stu or

Jason to deserve any punishment, let alone be set up for murder. Is she going to find out that some of this is her wrongdoing after all? She whispers, "I don't understand the package of cocaine."

"It was mostly powdered sugar. Stu and Jason didn't abandon a whole lot of product."

They abandoned me, though, thinks Lander.

The police tell her everything Miranda has gone through. Everything Miranda did for Lander's sake. Every wound she received.

Lander weeps again.

Her family did not abandon her.

Her parents were willing to sacrifice the cottage. Her grandmother sacrificed her home. And Miranda almost sacrificed her life.

Lander is thick with grief and shame.

She not only has misunderstood her own self. She has misunderstood what family is. Lander may test well, but Miranda gets it right.

The interviews go on and on. It's as hard for Lander to cooperate leaving jail as it was entering. But she answers everything. She is shocked by her cumulative bad judgment. Even more shocked to realize that she still loves Jason. How long will it take for that to pass?

And then the last door opens.

Lander walks into a room where her mother, her father and her sister race forward, beaming and shouting her name.

MONDAY MORNING

Miranda and her parents wait two hours for Lander to be processed out.

They're whiny about the delay and the officer at the front desk gets testy.

Miranda keeps thinking about Geoffrey. She never has properly thanked him, let alone admitted that she sees him so differently now. But how could she admit it? She can hardly say *I thought you were just a big lug without a brain.*

When the Allerdons get home, Geoffrey will eventually come over to swim off their dock. She will try to act normal and join him and then . . . then what?

Her parents call Grandma while they wait, telling her that Lander is innocent, will be coming home today, does not need an attorney. Thank you, thank you, thank you, but they will not need Grandma's house and money after all.

Grandma is a little deaf and shouts so loudly into her phone that Miranda hears her easily. Grandma's voice always makes her happy. "I don't care about the money!" yells Grandma. "You bring her to see me so I can tell for myself that she's all right."

Miranda's eyes blur with tears. I need to call Geoffrey, she thinks. Right now.

Miranda is not fond of phone calls. Texting is more fun; easier; less emotional.

She thinks of Geoffrey on Saturday and Sunday, walking back and forth so many times at the cottage. He wasn't just going home for lunch. He was checking on her, ready to be a big brother for her.

She is brave, but not brave enough to admit that she likes Geoffrey. And perhaps not as a big brother.

She composes a text: thank you Geoffrey for saving my life.

Seriously? She's going to thank him electronically? He's not even worth a few commas? Miranda gets a grip, deletes the unsent text and calls him.

"I'm so glad to hear from you!" says Geoffrey. "Are you okay? Is Lander okay? How are your parents doing? Are you coming back to the cottage or is it ruined for you? Is it true that you might sell it?"

And they are talking. Really talking, the way they never have. She fits in a thank-you, and then fits in another. It's like with Grandma, she realizes. You can never say enough thanks enough times, but the person who rescues you just wants to know if you're all right. "We'll probably drive to the cottage once they let Lander out," Miranda tells Geoffrey. "If we do, come on over. Maybe we can go out in the Zodiac for a while."

"I think you'll just want to be with Lander."

"Historically," says Miranda, "Lander's interest in me dwindles pretty fast."

It is lunchtime before Lander is out. At last, the whole family is in a parking lot without a single policeman. It is hard to get in the car because it is hard to stop hugging, and it is hard to snap seat belts because it is hard to be separated. Miranda's hand throbs, but she cannot take more pain meds if she wants to stay awake.

Lander looks awful. She is thin and gray and unclean. But she is the most beautiful thing they have ever seen. They pat her constantly, to reassure themselves that she's really back with them.

Lander looks cornered, even when she is safe in the backseat of their father's car. Whatever happened in that jail; whatever Lander saw when she was with Jason; whatever Lander saw inside herself—perhaps these things are too terrible to say out loud. Because Lander sidesteps all questions.

"I'm starving to death," Lander says instead. "I didn't eat a thing the whole time."

"Neither did we," says Miranda. "I'm totally starving."

Suddenly, the day feels kind of normal, which is amazing, considering they just experienced the most abnormal weekend in suburban America.

"Let's go to McDonald's!" cries Lander.

They stare at her. Lander is opposed to salt, grease and fast food.

Maybe it's all she can come up with, thinks Miranda. Maybe she's desperate for us to stop asking questions. She wants us to chew french fries instead. "I love McDonald's," says Miranda, supporting her sister.

Lander takes Miranda's hand, carefully checking to be sure it's the unhurt one. Tears leak out of Lander's eyes. "Oh, Rimmie, thank you. Thank you for everything."

"Miranda," she corrects automatically. She is thinking that Lander looks weak. Not weak from failure to eat. Weak from jail, horror, shame, fear.

She wonders how *she* would have done behind bars.

"Seriously? McDonald's?" asks their father, taking the turnpike exit that will lead them to the nearest one. "Plenty of real restaurants."

"I don't want to get out of the car," says Lander. "I don't want to face people. I don't even want to face myself yet."

Their parents exchange frightened looks.

"Until I've showered and fixed my hair," says Lander quickly. Their parents are pacified by this answer, but Miranda suspects that hair has little to do with it.

Bags of food and cardboard trays of drinks are passed into the car. Their father does not park but meanders along pretty shoreline roads rimmed with old stone walls, and they catch glimpses of the lighthouse. Lander is right. Hot food helps a lot. And Miranda loves everything salty.

Lander takes a deep breath. "I'm not going to medical school after all. You've spent too much money on me. I didn't understand how much. Or I understood and didn't care. You can't rack up more debt. I refuse to let you sell the cottage. I'm going to live at home for a few years. Earn money. Pay back everything. And besides, I need the time to think. I'm not who I thought I was."

There is a pause in which they consider the joy of keeping the cottage.

But Stu Crowder has done a vicious thing to the Allerdons and Miranda is not going to let him win. And Lander is a pretty quick thinker. She doesn't need two years to sort out her thoughts. Probably two afternoons will suffice.

"Oh, stop blubbering, Lander," says Miranda. "Of course you're going to medical school. You think we went through all this so you could run a donut franchise?"

"But what about *your* college costs? There's no money *now,* let alone after I've been in medical school. You saved me, Rimmie. How else do I repay you?"

Miranda does not believe that she can be repaid for what she has been through. Suffering isn't about payment anyway. You do what you have to do for your family.

"The medical school will probably agree to postpone my enrollment," Lander continues. "Meanwhile, we hang on to the cottage and I pay you back for my college bills."

It sounds good now, when Lander hasn't even showered jail off her body. But tomorrow? Next week? In fact, Lander's ordeal lasted only from Friday noon to Monday noon. Will Lander still feel like sacrificing a month from now? Miranda has her doubts.

But this decision is not in Miranda's hands.

She stares at the hand with the bandage. She, and not Lander, will carry the scar of this nightmare. It's a very small scar, when she considers how this could have ended.

Thank you, God.

When she can draw a steady breath, she says, "Let's drive on home. To the cottage. We need to see our river and know that there are no sharks in the water."

"Except there are," says Lander shakily. "There are sharks everywhere."

Miranda puts her arm around Lander. "And friends everywhere, too, Lanny. Except Willow. Drop Willow. She's worthless."

They bicker satisfyingly over the value of Willow.

Geoffrey sends a text. Coming?

She texts back. Soon.

ACKNOWLEDGMENTS

I am especially thankful to Beverly Horowitz, Rebecca Gudelis, and Elizabeth Harding for all their hard work.

The cottage in *No Such Person* is similar to a real house in Connecticut—left—where for many summers I mostly sat on the porch, admired the river, and read a lot of books.

To see more photographs of the cottage, the river, and tugs and barges, visit my Facebook page, carolinebcooneybooks.

ABOUT THE AUTHOR

Caroline B. Cooney is the author of *The Lost Songs; Three Black Swans; They Never Came Back; If the Witness Lied; Diamonds in the Shadow; A Friend at Midnight; Hit the Road; Code Orange; Goddess of Yesterday* (an ALA-ALSC Notable Children's Book); *The Ransom of Mercy Carter; Burning Up; The Face on the Milk Carton* (an IRA-CBC Children's Choice) and its companions, *Whatever Happened to Janie?* and *The Voice on the Radio* (each of them an ALA-YALSA Best Book for Young Adults), as well as *What Janie Found, What Janie Saw,* an ebook original story, and *Janie Face to Face; What Child Is This?* (an ALA-YALSA Best Book for Young Adults); *Driver's Ed* (an ALA-YALSA Best Book for Young Adults and a *Booklist* Editors' Choice); and *The Time Travelers,* Volumes I and II.

Caroline lives in South Carolina. Visit her online at carolinebcooneybooks.com.

Follow Caroline: